About the Author

Elissa Pepper has now been retired from the NHS for just over four years after working in the organisation for almost twenty. She joined as a secretary to the Head of Podiatry Services in the then Northamptonshire Heartlands PCT before going 'clinical' and working as a Physiotherapy Assistant at Kettering General Hospital.

Returning to the NHS after being a full-time carer to her mother for four years, she joined the Diabetic and High-Risk Foot Service as a Podiatry Assistant. Prior to joining the NHS, Elissa was PA to Financial and Managing Directors in the Foods, Logistics and Plastics Industries.

Elissa likes to keep busy and is a keen gardener, traveller, reader and, of course, an enthusiastic rambler.

WALKERS

ELISSA J Pepper

WALKERS

Vanguard Press

VANGUARD PAPERBACK

© Copyright 2025
Elissa J Pepper

The right of Elissa J Pepper to be identified as author of this work has been asserted by her in accordance with the Copyright, Designs and Patents Act 1988.

All Rights Reserved

No reproduction, copy or transmission of this publication may be made without written permission.
No paragraph of this publication may be reproduced, copied or transmitted save with the written permission of the publisher, or in accordance with the provisions of the Copyright Act 1956 (as amended).

Any person who commits any unauthorised act in relation to this publication may be liable to criminal prosecution and civil claims for damages.

A CIP catalogue record for this title is available from the British Library.

ISBN 978-1-83794-826-0

This is a work of fiction. Names, characters, businesses, places, events and incidents are either the products of the author's imagination or used in a fictitious manner. Any resemblance to actual persons, living or dead, or actual events is purely coincidental.

Vanguard Press is an imprint of
Pegasus Elliot Mackenzie Publishers Ltd.
www.pegasuspublishers.com

First Published in 2025

Vanguard Press
Sheraton House Castle Park
Cambridge England

Printed & Bound in Great Britain

Dedication

To all walkers, ramblers and hikers everywhere.

Acknowledgements

I wish to thank Tracy Cooper and Sue and Trevor Ottaway who read this book first and who all made constructive comments. You have encouraged me to continue writing.

The Carry on Walkers group to which I belong. What a smashing bunch of people you are! I so enjoy meeting up with you all every Tuesday morning to roam the wilds of Northamptonshire. Thank you all for your company.

According to the *Doomsday Book,* Stonechester had originally been a small Saxon settlement in the area of England, known as Norssex, comprising one wooden church (falling down), one mill (fallen down) by the River Pyddel (pronounced Pie-del but open to personal pronunciation), and three farms sharing some common land to graze sheep and cattle. The other land, devoted to strip farming, was notated as being full of weeds as well as inhabited by some rather bolshie natives who greatly objected to any 'snooping'; they apparently told William the Conqueror's commissioners to 'go forth and multiply' in the local Anglo Saxon local dialect.

The Romans had passed through some thousand years earlier; hence, the 'chester' from the Latin *castra* for camp but they did only camp for the three nights, because the then inhabitants stole all their food and weapons and threw stones at them. Hence, the name 'Stonechester'. Bizarrely, the red feathers in the centurions' helmets were also taken. Tacitus, the famous Roman historian and orator, noted in his famous *Historiae,* that the natives were last seen wearing them stuck to their bottoms, the red contrasting interestingly with their woad striped buttocks. Hence one could say, the Romans were experiencing Stonechester's version of an *anus horibilis*. Incidentally, red feathers and horizontal dark-blue and white stripes were later incorporated into Stonechester's coat of arms in celebration of a rare occasion when England had beaten Italy at something. Stonechester Harriers running club had taken this further as their athletes always wore red shorts with blue and white hooped singlets; their nickname was 'Woad Runners'.

After a bloody but, thankfully, brief encounter with the locals, the Vikings decided to leave well alone and not include Stonechester in the Danelaw. For many centuries, therefore, the inhabitants were left to rape and pillage each other in peace.

During the English Civil War, both sides made sure, they didn't stray into Stonechester and the surrounding countryside; Stonechester was a no-go area even then. That's why the Cavaliers and Roundheads fought their battle some twenty-five miles away at Naseby.

When the London to Sheffield railway line came through Stonechester and its surrounding environs in the mid-nineteenth century, the local menfolk got the navies drunk on their homemade brews and the womenfolk gave them STDs. Construction of the line was delayed by at least two months while the navies tried to recover or were laid off rather than laid.

Queen Victoria is rumoured to have passed through Stonechester on the royal train but like all previous visitors during the past two thousand years, she didn't stop for long. In her case, it was about twenty minutes whilst a flock of sheep was herded off the railway line with the train driver receiving a right royal mouthful from an irate shepherd.

With the arrival of the Industrial Revolution, new settlers, as well as the boot and shoe industry, came to Stonechester and, indeed, to the other large towns that had sprung up in the county of Norssex. Instead of passing through, people actually stayed. Stonechester thrived. This brought it in direct competition with the county town of Norssex: Norbrough. The inhabitants had mellowed somewhat by then, mellowed mainly by the money industry had brought to the area. But it appeared the money only stayed with certain local worthies who built rather palatial houses in Stonechester's town centre. For everybody else, two up, two down housing was deemed to be sufficient for their hoi polloi needs, but such building had encroached on hitherto purely agricultural land and, as the twentieth century progressed, more modern council housing expanded the town's boundaries further into the countryside. Then cheap foreign imports hit the local boot and shoe industry. Many factories closed down, workers were laid off and, with that, began Stonechester's decline into obscurity.

The local hospital, Stonechester General, which had started off as a little cottage hospital in the early twentieth century, had gradually expanded with the newest main building, all grey concrete, appearing in the '60s. The design was criticised; some called it an 'architectural sarcophagus'. By the '80s, it looked like a Soviet Bloc reject with its crumbling outer skin, large cracks and flaking paint. One local wag opined that it could end up in the Tate Modern, and rumour had it that Tracey Emin's unmade bed came from one of the wards.

It had been hoped that when Britain joined the Common Market, this decline would be halted. In an attempt at a trans-European Entente Cordiale, Stonechester was twinned with Merdique-sur-Seine in

France and Beschissheim-am-Main in Germany. After a brief exploratory visit to Stonechester, Merdique's Monsieur le Maire declared that his visit had been badly organised from beginning to end. Nobody – *absolument personne* – could speak a word of French, he and his wife had both suffered an upset stomach from eating fish and chips in a local restaurant at a lunch, held to celebrate British cuisine, and the members of the local council were bloody idiots – *imbéciles sanglants*. They didn't know their *'culs'* from their *'couloirs'*. He summed up their visit to Stonechester with a Gallic shrug of the shoulders and muttered, *"Ce sont les Stonechesteriens, ce sont les anglais."* He refused, for the safety of Merdique's inhabitants, to have anything more to do with Stonechester.

The Italian representative of a small town in Tuscany, who had accompanied the French to research the viability of twinning with Stonechester, left, as had his ancestors some two thousand years previously, in a state of shock.

The mayor of Beschissheim had also withdrawn his town from anything to do with Stonechester, primarily prompted to do so, following a football match between a Beschissheim eleven and a team from Stonechester. In a desire to emulate England's 1966 World Cup win over West Germany, the locals were determined to play some spirited football but were, of course, totally outplayed. Incensed to find themselves five nil down after twenty minutes, they fought back with some tough defensive play and even tougher tackling. By the end of the first half, Beschissheim were leading twelve nil, despite three of their players being carried off injured, and four Stonechester players receiving the red card, including their goalkeeper. There was also an altercation on the side lines between the Beschissheim and Stonechester's team managers, and a couple of punches were thrown. The two female police officers in attendance decided that enough was enough and that the match should be abandoned before it became too violent – also because the St John's ambulance crew had run out of bandages, analgesia and ice packs.

"Thank God, it wasn't a rugby match," remarked one of them later over a pint in his local. "It would've been World War Three."

When asked for his comments by Terry Bailey, the *Stonechester Gazette* reporter covering the match, the Stonechester team manager opined that the match had been very close indeed, 'the lads' had done really well but the ref was a berk and the assistant refs were blind. "If there'd been a second 'alf," he said, holding a handful of tissues to his bleeding nose. "We could've won it. We were wobbed."

Stonechester Brexited in September, 2011.

The twenty-first century brought further downturns in the local economy. The High Street, once full of independent shops and businesses as well as the usual well-known chain stores, so bustling, interesting and busy, was nowadays devoid of life – and shops – unless you were in need of a vape, tattoo, charity shop clothing, a mobile phone or cheap washing powder. The market square in front of the church (now built of stone) was empty of stalls but full of broken bottles, polystyrene takeaway boxes, squashed beer cans and other detritus. Nowadays, the only people to be found in the High Street were drunks, druggies and half a dozen bewildered-looking asylum seekers in search of a lorry to smuggle them back to France. As one local noted wryly, "The only thing missing is tumbleweed blowing down the High Street."

Another added, "And Clint Eastwood and his jingling spurs and cigar."

A third asked, "Where's Mary Portas?"

At least, Stonechester was sufficiently large enough nowadays for Royal Mail to give the town and the surrounding area its own postcode: 'SZ'.

So, when a Year 12 pupil at a local secondary school inadvertently wrote *Doomsday Book* in his History homework essay, *"What did the Normans do in Stonechester?"* his teacher agreed that this summed up the town to a tee.

January, 2018

It had finally stopped raining. Douglas Yardley-Henderson got out of his silver Range Rover and tutted when he saw how bespattered and muddy it was. The road leading up here onto the wold was a nightmare when it rained. He went to the back of the Range Rover and retrieved his wellington boots; he was going to need them up here. The ground was so saturated, it was like trying to walk through dark-brown glue. He pulled the boots on, ensuring that the trouser bottoms of his Gieves & Hawkes suit were carefully tucked in. As he straightened up, he heard a beep beep and looking around, saw Councillor Fred Denton pull up behind in a black Series 5 BMW. Douglas raised his hand in recognition and waited until Fred got out.

"I hope you've got a pair of wellies, Fred. It's a real swamp up here."

"Yeah, I have." Fred, being rather rotund, huffed and puffed as he slowly pulled on his boots. Douglas began to lose patience. After all, time was money. His money, actually.

"Right, come on. You've got the plans with you, I believe. Let's have a look now we're up here." Fred, still recovering from the exertion of pulling on a pair of wellington boots over his fat calves puffed again, as he bent forwards to pull out a roll of A0 size paper from the back seat of the BMW. Between the two of them, they unrolled it, rested it on the bonnet of the BMW and looked over towards the wold stretching away into the murky distance.

"So, the plan is to buy the wold and sell it to companies for large scale warehousing and logistics." Douglas pointed at the bottom of the plan. "Here's the A6 coming off the A14. It's dual carriageway all the way to Stonechester and beyond, so no problem with access. All the warehousing is modular so that won't take long to construct. It'll just be the access off the A6 onto the wold itself, continuing along the river valley and the utilities that'll take all the time and the money. Mind, we can also build a solar panel power plant which will provide the electrics. That's going to be a big selling point, Fred. Universal Energy is really interested in doing that. I've already started making some contacts in some really big outfits in the logistics sector, and there's a lot of interest. After all, local housing is pretty cheap because no bastard really wants to live here." Douglas gave a cynical laugh. "Can't say I blame them. Stonechester's a real shithole."

"It's not that bad, Doug," said Fred. "There's far worse places, you know."

"Really? If you say so, but then, as leader of the Stonechester Borough Council, and a member of Norssex County Council, you would say that." Fred went to say something but Douglas continued flattening out the plan with one hand and pointing with the other towards some landmarks that were still visible in the gloom. "This area is for that solar panel plant. As you can see, it is right beside the mere. The access road will come off the A6 at the Blackbird Roundabout and run between them and the first warehouse with branch roads running off that to the other warehouses." He pointed to the top of the plan. "The main access road will then run right over the wold down to the valley below to finish where it joins the A510 here." He looked at Fred. "All the council has to do now is to get those two owners to sell."

Fred sighed. "Easier said than done, Doug. Old man Drage will be a tough nut to crack but Chris Tilley will sell now that his dad died and left him the farm. He's not interested in farming. He wants to bugger off to Spain or somewhere with a nice tidy sum."

"Well, you know them, Fred, so I'll leave them to your undoubted powers of persuasion." Douglas sounded faintly sarcastic and his tone was not lost on Fred.

"I'll have a chat to both of them. Leave it with me, Doug."

"I'll have to, Fred. But remember this: you and I are in line to make an absolute packet out of this lot. I'm not talking thousands; it'll be a couple of million each. You'll be able to clear all your gambling and other debts and have all the girlfriends – or boyfriends – you want. Think about that when you talk to them." Douglas turned away and began to roll up the plans. Fred shot a quick look of sheer hatred at Douglas's back before managing to compose his facial features.

"Here's the plan; you keep them." Douglas handed them to Fred. "Keep me posted on the sales."

"Will do. Anything else?"

"No, that's it. You can leave now. I just want to have a walk around up here before it rains again."

"Right. OK. Speak soon then." Fred got back into his BMW without bothering to remove his wellingtons. He raised his hand before driving off, but Douglas didn't bother looking back at him. He began walking down the muddy track but soon turned back as it started raining again. As he removed his wellingtons and put on his bespoke leather shoes, he fervently hoped Fred Denton would be successful in negotiating decent selling prices. Really, the guy was a self-made idiot.

***

Stonechester was surrounded by quite a few villages that, like itself, had grown in size during the past two centuries but, unlike itself, had remained stubbornly rural and agricultural. Three villages, in particular, were clustered along the River Pyddel. Upper Pyddelham was sited near to the outskirts of Stonechester; a narrow strip of woodland separated it from the latest private estate of executive pixie housing. It was well known for its pub, the Cat and Cradle, which offered the local ales and micro distillery produced gin, together with bistro food – all at fine dining prices. Middle Pyddelham was another village some three miles further along the River Pyddel and, in the main, still retained its original seventeenth- and eighteenth-century houses. The locals affectionately referred to it as 'Middle Piddle'. Lower Pyddelham, about four miles further along the river, was the elite village in the area. The manor house was early seventeenth century, its grounds beautifully cultivated by the current owners, Brigadier General (Retired) Sir Henry and Lady Caroline Fryers-Faversham. The rest of the houses in the village had been built no later than the late nineteenth century and their gardens mirrored those of the manor house: they were immaculately maintained.

Most of the residents of Middle and Lower Pyddelham were retired, enjoying the benefits of country life courtesy of various Statins, Ramipril, Omeprazole and Furosemide and, occasionally, Dulcolax. Younger, aspiring people still working were mainly domiciled in Upper Pyddelham and, of course, in Stonechester itself.

The three villages were served by St Agatha's in Lower Pyddelham, a church dating from the late fifteenth century. It had been built in thanks by the then villagers who had survived the Black Death; previously, the area had been staunchly pagan. The current vicar, the Reverend Michael Fuller, lived with his sister, Barbera, in the rectory, next door. Both were heavily involved in the doings of all three villages, especially during any festivals, intervening when tempers tended to become frayed as parishioners fell out over the flower arrangements and argued about the tea and coffee making rotas.

The countryside surrounding these villages was still being farmed, but there was a plethora of footpaths and bridle ways, offering easy rambles and ambles with minimal gradients. The best views were from the top of the wold, a remote and substantial area of land rising out of the Pyddel Valley, comprising heavy clay, shale and sandstone. It was an anomaly in the gently undulating landscape, looking south across the Pyddel Valley, with Stonechester a haze to the east and, to the south and west, rolling meadows and fields blurring into the horizon. The wold itself could be pretty bleak in winters; the wind whipping across it as there were no trees as such to act as a windbreak. The more fertile parts of it were under plough having been farmed by the Drage and Tilley families from time out of mind, but it was really an unofficial nature reserve, attracting all sorts of birds and animals. A small mere, fed by various springs and streams, offered a good supply of water for all the wildlife.

Ramblers, horse riders, nature lovers and bird watchers, as well as those inhabitants wishing to express their *passion al fresco,* had been visiting the area regularly for generations. Generally speaking, it hadn't changed much in the last three hundred years.

July, 2018

It was a beautiful Friday evening, and Reverend Michael Fuller and his sister, Barbera, decided to go for a walk across the wold. Reverend Fuller was feeling happy and relaxed; he had finished writing Sunday's sermon, a task he always found rather onerous.

They set off, initially following the line of the Pyddel, and then turned north along a bridleway that climbed out of the valley towards the top of the wold. The views from there were beautiful: gently undulating fields of ripening wheat, sprinkled with copses and the odd farm building. The sun, now lowering towards the horizon, was sending the last of its warming rays across the land, highlighting any rises with gold and dappling the River Pyddel with shimmering silver. The only blot on this visual idyll was the outskirts of Stonechester to the east, a mixture of warehousing, houses and tiny cars speeding along the A14.

Ignoring the grey smudge of modern living that was Stonechester, Reverend Fuller remarked on the beauty of the view. Barbera nodded in agreement.

"Let's just walk over the wold to the mere and then back again," she suggested. "This evening is too lovely to waste." They set off again northwards towards the mere. As they approached it, they were overtaken by six riders who galloped past them and also past a red Volvo parked by the mere with both back doors open.

"Well, those riders will have frightened off any wildlife. If the owner of that car is a twitcher, then they're going to be most unimpressed," remarked Reverend Fuller.

"Perhaps, the car's been abandoned. Look, the back doors are open," observed Barbera. They both strolled towards the Volvo to investigate and stopped. It was gently rocking and the windscreen had steamed up. Suddenly, two heads appeared parallel to the ground, followed by the top half of their bodies.

"The earth moved!" a woman cried. "Oh, darling, it moved and I heard thunder." Since her partner's face was captured between her large breasts, he was unable to comment – or breathe. Suddenly the woman caught sight of the Fullers and screamed loudly, trying to push him from her. Her partner raised his head to discover the cause of her distress, bashed it on the top of the door frame and his face promptly disappeared back between the woman's breasts.

"I think it's best we leave, Michael," said Barbera. "Now." They turned and retraced their steps at pace but in silence. Behind them they heard the Volvo's engine start up. It passed them at speed and disappeared down the track towards the valley.

I do hope that man didn't hurt his head too badly, mused Reverend Fuller when they reached the rectory.

October, 2018

"Well, Fred. What did he say?" Douglas Yardley-Henderson leant back in his black leather, ergonomic chair, and tucked his mobile more comfortably under his right ear whilst he added milk and sugar to his freshly cafetière'd coffee.

"Good news, Doug. Chris Tilley's very willing to sell but wants another ten grand on top of what we offered." Fred Denton sounded tentative.

"No, that's OK. I can go with that. What's another ten grand in the scheme of things." Douglas sipped his coffee. "Get all the paperwork done and signed off asap. The quicker it's all completed, the better. What about Ted Drage?"

Fred hesitated and Douglas, guessing what was coming next, sighed. "Well?"

"I had a long chat with him, Doug. I really did try my best to get him to agree to a sale, but he said he and his family have farmed that land for a couple of centuries and he didn't want to be the one to…"

"Oh for Chrissakes, Fred! He's got no family to speak of, so who's going to get the farm?"

"Apparently, there's a long-lost cousin or someone. He's made a will and has left it to this person. He wouldn't tell me who it is so we can't contact them." Douglas sighed again.

"Right then, Fred. This is what you do. You make an appointment for us both to see him. Leave it for a couple of weeks and then ring him and invite him to lunch somewhere. Let's see if both of us can persuade him to sell."

"He's a stubborn bastard, Doug, and he's not daft."

"I thought that might be the case. Meanwhile, I'll arrange for some background digging to see if he's been a naughty boy. You know, diddling the tax man and that sort of thing. Do you know of anything we can use to, er, persuade him?"

"Not really." Douglas gritted his teeth. Really, Fred was a total zero at times. He needed a good kick up the arse.

"Fred, try and be a bit more proactive. Ask around. Chat to people. You were born and bred in Stonechester, weren't you?"

"OK, Doug. I'll see what I can find." Fred sounded unenthusiastic.

"Yeah, you do that small thing, Fred. Let me know immediately you find anything. Bye." Douglas slapped his mobile against his thigh in frustration. Fred Denton was a total waste of space but he had his uses. At least, the Tilley guy was going to sell so that was something. The Tilley land, adjacent to the wold, would accommodate the solar panels and two of the planned six warehouses, but it was the Drage land that would be the cherry on top. Four warehouses and the main access road off the A6 were planned to be built on it. Douglas thought for a moment and then used his mobile. The number rang twice before it was answered.

"Hallo." A man's voice.

"It's me," said Douglas. "I've got some work for you. I want you to do some digging."

December, 2018

"Merry Christmas, Mr Drage. Or may I call you Ted?" Douglas raised his glass of St Emilion in a toast. Ted Drage looked at him and then at Fred Denton who had raised his pint of IPA. He picked up his pint of Guinness.

"Merry Christmas," he growled and took a large mouthful, looking around at the very unfamiliar surroundings of the Cat and Cradle bistro restaurant; he had only ever been in the saloon bar previously.

"May I call you Ted?" Douglas repeated.

"Yes." Douglas waited for a moment in case Ted decided to add a few more words. He didn't.

"Please, order whatever you want from the menu," offered Douglas. "What are you having, Fred?"

"Er, the steak, I think."

"Make that two," said Ted.

"Make that three," added Douglas smiling. He waved over to the waiter who was hovering. "Three steaks. Mine medium rare please." He looked at the other two.

"Well done for me," said Ted.

"Ditto," Fred agreed. The waiter disappeared.

"Well now, Ted. I bet you know why myself and Fred invited you here today."

"Yes." Douglas waited again to see if Ted was going to elaborate further, but he picked up his Guinness and took another mouthful. Douglas inwardly sighed. This was going to be bloody hard work.

"So-oo. Ted. We want to buy your land. If the reason you are unwilling to sell is because of money, we can offer more, although our offer is a good one. Is money the problem?" Ted was looking long and hard at Douglas who was frankly finding his stare off putting.

"No," Again the curt reply. Douglas was beginning to lose patience. "What is the problem?"

"That land has been in my family for generations." Well, at least, Ted wasn't totally monosyllabic; he could string some words into a sentence.

"We understand that, Ted, we really do, but you don't have any family to pass it on to."

"I got a niece and it's willed to her."

"Is that Miss Felicity Holmes, currently living in London? I believe she was your wife's sister's only child and, currently, she's a hairdresser." Ted sat up straighter in his chair.

"How d'you know that?" Douglas smiled.

"Oh, Fred here has ways and means to find out these things." Douglas's smile grew wider. "Just like we found out that you've been illegally claiming grants from the EC before we brexited and now from Defra. You also occasionally handle stolen farm machinery." Fred choked on his IPA and spluttered into his napkin. Ted stared at Douglas.

"You got no proof."

"Want to bet, Ted?" At this point, their conversation was interrupted by the arrival of their meal. Once the waiter had left them, Douglas continued as if Ted had never spoken.

"We have a video of a tractor in your yard being stripped down for spares. Its plates are not registered to you. Also, we had a chat with one of your, er, customers. A Joe Harvey." Douglas emphasised 'customers'. "Apparently, you have quite a lucrative sideline there." Douglas cut a slice of steak, popped it into his mouth and chewed appreciatively. "Very good. What's yours like Ted?" Ted was still staring at him. "Lost your appetite? What a shame!" Douglas took a sip of his wine. "Mmm, not bad. Not bad at all. By the way, Ted, we noticed that you always seem to pay cash for everything. Quite unusual nowadays although I would imagine all that grant money you receive comes by cheque, so you'd have to have a bank account."

Ted Drage continued to sit in silence without touching his food. Fred had already finished and was downing his pint of IPA, eyeing Ted's plate. *Really,* Douglas thought. *Fred is an absolute pig and in line for a TOTY (Twat of the Year) award.*

"So, Ted. We'd like to buy your land. Shall we talk money? Then hopefully, you'll enjoy your steak before it gets too cold and before Fred eats it."

February, 2019

Brian Ramsbottom was up on the wold alone today, hidden in a small hide and well wrapped up against the sleet and cold east wind. He was watching a robin through his Zeiss binoculars, its red breast startingly bright and cheerful against the browns and greys of the leafless hawthorn hedge. The silence was suddenly broken by the sound of a vehicle struggling up the muddy track, leading onto the wold, and the bird, startled, flew off. Brian swore roundly and watched as a 4 x 4 came to a halt not far away. Four men got out and decanted several aluminium cases from its rear. Two of the men began setting up theodolites whilst the other two started unwinding fluorescent yellow tape and unpacking various pieces of kit from the cases.

"What the…" Brian muttered. Then, the penny dropped. This was for a survey of some kind. *Shit!* he thought. *They're going to build something up here! Bugger that for a game of soldiers.* He crawled out of his hide and walked over to the nearest man who was crouched over one of the cases. Since Brian was sporting green and brown camouflage gear, he blended nicely into the landscape.

"Excuse me," said Brian, tapping the man's shoulder. The man fell backwards into a particularly muddy patch of scrub.

"Jesus, you frit the life out me!" he yelped. The other men looked around.

"Who are you lot?" asked Brian. "What're you doing up here?"

"We've been contracted to carry out a preliminary survey of this area preparatory to applying for outline planning permission to build warehousing up here. Who the bloody hell are you?" one of them asked. The man on the ground had now been helped upright by one of his colleagues.

"I live locally and come up here to do bird watching and if you build here, you'll destroy some wonderful wildlife habitats."

"Well sorry about that, mate, but that's how it is. Now, if you don't mind, we'll get on with the survey." All four of them ignored Brian and continued unpacking and setting up their equipment.

"We'll see about that, sunshine," muttered Brian. He returned to the hide and collected his belongings.

"Yeah, we'll see about that."

***

"You're joking, Brian!" Len Sharman, landlord of the Cat and Cradle Pub, Upper Pyddelham's centre for the latest local news and gossip and over the top prices, paused his pulling of a pint of Red Devil, a local ale brewed, rumour had it, in a cauldron.

"No, I'm bloody not, Len." Brian turned to the other people surrounding the bar. "Wish I was. It's not even homes; it's going to be warehouses, the guy said. That'll mean new roads for access and more traffic. It's going to drive off all the wildlife up there." There was a murmur of agreement and sympathy from his fellow patrons.

Len resumed pulling Brian's pint. "Here you go, Brian. Get that down you, mate."

"Cheers, Len." Brian took a long draught and put his nearly empty glass down on the bar. He turned to a well-dressed man sitting beside him.

"Do you know anything about this, Mike? You're a legal beagle, aren't you?"

Mike Culverhouse was a senior partner in a firm of Norbrough solicitors, Messrs Coleman, James & Wright. He sipped his gin and tonic before replying, "No, this is news to us all, I believe. As far as I know, there's been nothing in the council minutes. As for myself, Brian, I deal in family law but let me get one of my conveyancing solicitors to make a few enquiries with the land registry and the council. I think it's about time that this was brought into the public domain. I, personally, would be very sorry if the wold is spoiled in any way. My wife and I enjoy walking up there. She's a member of the Stonechester and District Wellbeing Walking Club and is going to be well peed off when this news gets out. In fact, a lot of people like going up there, if not for walking, then there are other pursuits." He raised an eyebrow and grinned.

Len said, "My wife's a member of the club, too. She's going to be furious. Well, I'm Stonechester born and bred, and I can remember all around here as being fields and meadows. Rita and I used to do our courting up there. We used to cycle out here and swim in the Pyddel and go blackberrying up on the wold. Stonechester used to be a small market town then but nowadays? Well, the missus don't even bother going there to shop no more unless she has to. Mind you, the shopping mall has improved things a bit and there's that new café opened in Meeting Lane but the High Street is a real dump, especially since Marks & Spencer and Woolworths went. The last thing we need is warehouses on what is a beautiful countryside." There was another murmur of agreement from everyone.

"Leave it with me," said Mike Culverhouse, taking a large sip of his G&T. "I'll let you know what I discover."

***

"Oh, Len, surely not!" Rita Sharman stared at her husband, shocked. "They can't do that, can they?"

"Well, it's what Brian Ramsbottom was saying in the bar, earlier." Len shrugged. "Right bloody shame if it's true."

"But our walking club goes up there frequently. It's lovely and wild except where Ted's land is, of course. This is rural feudalism!"

"You mean vandalism, love. I told Mike you'd be angry."

"Angry! I'm bloody curious!"

"You mean furious, love." Rita ignored him and continued her tirade. "I'm going to phone the rest of the walkers and tell them. Mandy Culverhouse is a walker too, so she'll make sure Mike keeps his word and does some digging."

"Well ring them tomorrow because it's almost midnight. I'm whacked and I'm going to bed." With that, he disappeared upstairs. Rita reached for her mobile and began to type in *WhatsApp*.

***

An Extraordinary General Meeting of the Stonechester and District Wellbeing Walking Club took place three days later, in St Agatha's Church, Lower Pyddeham. The Wellbeing Walkers had also been joined by members of the Stonechester Historical Society, the local Yoga and Keep Fit Group, Stonechester and District Cyclists (collectively known as SaD2C), Stonechester WI, the Stonechester Community Library's Knit and Natter Club, members of the Pyddel Valley Twitchers and Birders Club and sundry members of Weight Watchers and Slimmer's World who had joined the Wellbeing Walkers in order to try and lose weight, as well as the local horse-riding fraternity, the latter bringing into the church a strong odour of the stables.

Reverend Michael Fuller had never seen his church so full of people. Alas, though, not to worship. He had given permission for its use to Barbera, a member of the Historical Society and an occasional Walker. Barbera was doing sterling work at the tea urn, dispensing welcome and drinks in equal quantities. When everybody had a drink and were seated in the pews, Lady Caroline Fryers-

Faversham, another staunch member of the Historical Society, climbed the steps into the pulpit and leaned her comely bulk towards her audience. She gave the appearance of an avenging angel, a female John Knox. Everyone stopped talking.

"Ladies and gentlemen," she began. "I would like to thank all of you for coming here today. I know the Wellbeing Walkers usually hold their meetings at a coffee shop in town." She nodded and smiled at Rita Sharman and Mandy Culverhouse. "But Reverend Fuller has kindly consented to our meeting here today in this house of God." She smiled and nodded at both Michael and Barbera. "Thank you, Reverend." She continued – her hands gripping the edge of the pulpit, "We are meeting here, because our beautiful wold, our beautiful Pyddel Valley is in danger of disappearing under warehouses and access roads. If this happens, ladies and gentlemen, it would be monstrous. Indeed, it would be tantamount to rural rape!" There was complete silence and a collective intake of breath. Rape was not a word one tended to hear in a church.

"We must do something to prevent this happening and…"

"How do you know that there's going to be building on the wold?" Everyone turned to stare at the very brave man who had dared dam Lady Caroline's flow. He stood up, making it easier for her to glare at him. Suddenly, "Because my Brian was up on the wold, birdwatching, when some surveyors appeared with a load of kit and started measuring up or whatever surveyors do." This from Lorraine Ramsbottom. She also stood up and glancing at Lady Caroline, added, "They told Brian that they'd come to make a preliminary survey for outline planning permission for warehousing." She sat down again. The man sat down, too.

"Fortunately for us," continued Lady Caroline, as if there had been no interruptions. "We were able to obtain help from a member of the legal profession. Mrs Culverhouse, would you like to explain." Since Lady Caroline showed no signs of descending from the pulpit, Mandy stood up in her pew and surveyed her audience.

"My husband is a senior partner in a firm of solicitors in Norbrough. When he heard from Brian Ramsbottom what had happened up on the wold, he got one of the conveyancers to run a check with the land registry and to do some digging generally." She sighed. "Yes, it's true."

"How do you mean true?" This is from the same man who had earlier challenged Lady Caroline. Mandy looked at him impatiently and then at everyone else. Rita continued on her behalf, "The land owned by the Tilley family has been sold to a spell company in London."

"Shell company, she means," interrupted Mandy. "The Tilleys owned all the land leading up to the wold and the Drages own and farm a lot of the wold itself. To make any building or warehousing viable, this company would have to buy the Drage land, too."

"There were some guys on Chris Tilley's land a couple of weeks ago, doing some sort of measuring." This from Susan Sudborough, one of the Historical Society members. "I thought they were doing some sort of archaeology. You know, like *Time Team* used to do on Channel 4. I remember thinking 'good' because I'm sure there's remains up there. Buildings, I mean, not people." She sat up straighter in her pew. "Although, you never know, do you." She turned to her fellow Historical Society colleagues squashed in along the pew for support. Lady Caroline tutted from above, "Ted Drage won't sell. It'd be over his dead body," opined Julia Carrington-Herbert, proprietor of Ride Well Stables, cutting across the musings of the Historical Society members. "I asked him last year if we could hack over one of his fields when it was only stubble and he said no, because his family had farmed it for centuries, and it wasn't going to be used as a bloody racecourse. His words, not mine," she added.

"Doesn't something like this get put out to public consultation?" asked one of the cyclists.

"Yes, it does," agreed Mandy. "But a lot of the time, the public is ignored, especially where big money's concerned."

"Ain't that the truth?" somebody else called out. There was a consensual nodding in the pews. Lady Caroline had become impatient at being ignored.

"Are we going to do something?" she boomed from her perch.

***

Looking back at that first PVP (Pyddel Valley Protesters) meeting in St Agatha's, Reverend Fuller's heart was filled with pride that so many, so diverse and so disparate a people could come together to work for benefit of their community. The meeting had agreed that Mandy Culverhouse and Rita Sharman keep them briefed about any new developments that they and their husbands discovered in their respective line of work. Lorraine Ramsbottom was tasked with asking Brian to get his younger twitchers to report any suspicious activity around the valley and on the wold, in case the retired members forgot to do so. Lastly, everybody gave Barbera Fuller their mobile numbers so that she could set up at PVP *WhatsApp* group.

Barbera agreed with Michael when he spoke about the wonderful community spirit they had both witnessed. They both prayed for a successful outcome during Evensong. As Barbera remarked, if divine intervention couldn't help them, then nothing could.

April, 2019

Felicity Holmes, manageress of the 'Hair Fair' Salon de Coiffure, Stoke Newington Church Street, London, N16 sighed inwardly. She was having a dreadful day at work and, surely, it couldn't get worse, or could it? One of the trainee hairdressers had managed to take a slice out of her finger with some scissors and Felicity had had to call for a taxi to take her to the local A & E to have it stitched. The taxi driver had not been impressed. "It makes me back seat look like a bleedin' crime scene," he moaned. Then one of the customers complained bitterly that her perm had made her look like a French poodle and wanted her money back. After that was sorted out, it was discovered the timer on one of the hair dryers was faulty. The customer had emerged from under it twenty minutes later than she should have done. The protective hairnet had almost disintegrated, and the curlers were red hot. It had taken Felicity, two other hairdressers, and copious amounts of warm water, quite some time to remove these items from the woman's head. When she was able to talk again, the woman explained that she had realised something was wrong when there was a funny smell, and she had been trying to get somebody's attention – unsuccessfully – until one of the staff had noticed the smell, too. The resulting coiffure resembled the surface of a scouring pad, especially as the extra heat had turned the promised autumn russet lowlights to bright green highlights.

So, it was with great relief that she locked up the salon just after 6:30 p.m. and caught the bus number 149 to her small, rented flat in Edmonton. There was some post on the mat, and she went through it whilst waiting for the kettle to boil for tea. There was a bill from Thames Water, some leaflets advertising various products and a large A4 envelope. Felicity opened the latter, her curiosity piqued, and drew out a large wad of paper. The covering letter from Messrs Harding, Russell, Solicitors, Stonechester, announced the demise of her uncle, Edward Anthony Drage, the previous month. According to his will, she was sole beneficiary. A copy of his last will and testament was enclosed. Could she, therefore, ring the above telephone number to make an appointment to discuss what was now her 'inheritance'.

The kettle had come to a boil. It switched itself off with a smart click but Felicity continued to stare at the letter. Uncle Ted. She forgot the last time she saw him. He was her mum's brother-in-law and what she could remember of him was not exactly inspiring. *He lived on a farm outside a small town in, now where was it? Oh yeah. Stone something. Somewhere right in the sticks.* She used to go and stay there in the school holidays when her aunt, his wife and her mum's sister, was alive, but that had all stopped when Aunty Viv died. Felicity sighed and shrugged. Oh well, it was worth ringing up about, wasn't it? She'd probably been left the farm. She could always sell that.

Felicity switched the kettle back on and put a teabag in a mug. When the water had boiled again, she poured it into the mug and waited for it to steep. *Yeah,* she thought. *I'll give them a ring tomorrow.*

***

"What do you mean he's dead!" Douglas Yardley-Henderson glared at Fred Denton. They were meeting at their usual spot up on the wold. Fred had rung Douglas earlier and said they had to speak urgently.

"It's not my bloody fault, Doug!" Fred flared back. "The guy died on the 29th of March – massive stroke, apparently. Postman found him outside his front door and phoned for an ambulance. Nothing could be done though."

"So, the bastard never signed any papers then. Christ Almighty!" Douglas slapped the bonnet of his Range Rover in anger and frustration, then grimaced as the pain shot up his arm. "Jesus, Fred, my investors won't wait forever."

Fred had made sure his BMW was sited between himself and Douglas before he broke this latest information. "Well, there is some good news, Doug. Apparently, he willed the farm and the land to his niece, I'm reliably informed. Harding, Russell is handling his estate."

"Do we know anything about this niece?" Douglas glared at Fred.

"Yeah, she lives somewhere in North London. She's the only beneficiary."

"Are you absolutely sure?"

Fred sighed. "Yes, I am. My informant" – he emphasised on 'informant' – "is reliable. She's a hairdresser. The niece, I mean, not my informant."

This seemed to calm Douglas down, much to Fred's relief. He asked, "What else do you know about her?"

"She's single, no kids or partners or such like as far as we can tell. She's got an appointment with one of the senior probate managers, next week."

"Right, well make sure your 'informant' keeps you, well, informed. The probate process shouldn't take too long if everything is all legal and above board. I want to know immediately when everything has gone to her and then we can make our move. I bloody well hope she isn't as thick as shit as her uncle was."

Fred shrugged. "I'll let you know as soon as I know, Doug."

"Yeah, Fred, just make sure you do."

***

Felicity Holmes was the only passenger who got off the train at Stonechester railway station. Amazingly, the train was on time. At the entrance, there were four taxis parked up in a line, waiting for business. She tapped on the side window of the first one and the driver, who had been deeply engrossed in page three of the *Daily Mirror,* was visibly startled at the sight of her face against the glass. Clutching his heart with his left hand, he wound down the side window with his right.

"Can you take me to Harding, Russell, the solicitors, please. They're in the Broadway."

"Yeah, yeah. Get in, love. Bloody 'ell, you did make me jump."

"Sorry." Felicity got in and belted herself in on the back seat. The taxi chugged off and three minutes later, dropped her off outside a sombre, red building that may have been a des res in the early twentieth century but now looked dark and foreboding. Felicity paid the driver his fee of £10 and the taxi disappeared back down the street in a puff of black exhaust fumes. Making a mental note to walk back to the station and save herself another tenner, she entered through a glass door into a bright, modern and tastefully decorated reception area. The receptionist looked up and smiled.

"May I help you?"

Felicity introduced herself and was asked to take a seat. She had just made herself comfortable on the extremely comfortable leather sofa when a smartly dressed woman of around forty years emerged from a door on the right.

"Miss Holmes? Hi, my name is Christiana Morleigh, Senior Probate Manager." She held out her hand to Felicity who shook it. "I'm pleased to meet you. Do come this way."

She led Felicity through the door and along a corridor. She stopped outside 'Meeting Area 2' and ushered Felicity into another tastefully appointed room.

"Please make yourself comfortable, Miss Holmes. Tea or coffee?"

Felicity sat down in one of the deep armchairs.

"Oh, er, coffee please. Milk, no sugar. Thank you." Christiana picked up a phone and asked for two coffees. She sat down in an armchair opposite Felicity and picked up a file from the coffee table between them.

"Well, first of all, many thanks for coming here today for this meeting. I hope you had a good journey."

"Yes, I did, thank you. I…"

There was a knock on the door and Christiana got up to admit a young girl carrying a tray with two coffees and a plate of biscuits. She placed it on the table, handed Felicity her coffee and left.

"Right, now we can start." Christiana sat down and opened the file. "First of all, our condolences on the death of your uncle, Miss Holmes. He had been a client of ours for many years. Did you have much to do with him at all? I notice you live in London."

"Well, no, not really. I used to come and stay on the farm during the school holidays when Aunty Viv was alive but after she died, we all lost touch." Felicity sipped her coffee, adding, "Aunty Viv was my mum's sister and married to Ted, you see."

"Yes, I can see that from his file." Christiana glanced at the file again. "Well, Miss Holmes, you are sole beneficiary and are in line to inherit Mr Drage's estate that comprises farm buildings and equipment, about thirty hectares of land and around £100,000 in savings with the Norssex Building Society. Naturally, probate will take some time and… Miss Holmes, are you OK?"

Felicity thought she was going to faint. She took a deep breath to steady herself but had to exhale speedily.

"Are you OK?" repeated Christiana. Felicity gulped.

"Er, yes, I think so. It's a bit of a shock, you see." She picked up her coffee cup with shaking hands and took a sip. "I never expected all that, Ms Morleigh." She cradled the cup between her trembling hands, trying not to spill its contents.

"No, I suppose not. I'm sorry it is a shock but not an unpleasant one, I hope." Felicity shook her head.

"No, but honestly, it's such a lot of money. Just his savings alone." Christiana smiled, sympathetically.

"Well, if you decide to sell the land, Miss Holmes, you would certainly get a good price for it. Land in the Stonechester area is in high demand for housing and planning permission has already been given for warehousing and light industry, I believe, to the north of the town. You could well end up being a very wealthy woman."

"Yes, I suppose so."

"No supposing about it, Miss Holmes." Christiana referred to the file again. "As I was saying, all this has to go through probate, the land registry and all the other legal procedures necessary for the estate to come to you in its entirety, less any legal fees, of course." She coughed apologetically. "Which brings me to ask whether you are happy for Harding, Russell to handle the probate on your behalf."

"Yes, that's fine by me. I wouldn't know where to begin." Christiana immediately became more business-like. She retrieved a thin wad of papers from the file. "These are our terms of business. Please sign here and here and here and on the last page. You may borrow my pen." She handed Felicity a very expensive top of the range Parker ballpoint. While Felicity signed on the dotted lines, Christiana toyed with a long thin silver letter opener, a satisfied smile smugly settling across her sharp features.

***

Walking back to the railway station, Felicity felt she was in some kind of dream. How different from her trip to Stonechester to attend Uncle Ted's funeral, a few weeks ago. It had poured with rain all day; thankfully, he had been cremated with only Felicity and a couple of his friends in attendance. Since Harding, Russell had arranged the funeral, as per her uncle's will, this would also be deducted from his estate, Christiana had explained.

After the funeral, the two friends had come over to introduce themselves, but a third man sitting at the back of the hall had disappeared. One, a rather portly, older man said his name was Fred Denton and the other younger one introduced himself as Douglas Yardley-Henderson. Both offered their condolences for her loss. Douglas gave her his business card, explaining that he had been in discussion with her uncle about buying the farm. Perhaps, once her inheritance had been settled, she could give him a ring.

She arrived at the station to find that the train back to London was due in ten minutes. Grinning to herself, she went to the ticket office and bought an upgrade to first class.

***

The man who had sat at the back at Ted Drage's funeral had returned to London and was sitting in one of the offices at the Serious Fraud Office building in Cockspur Street. He had just taken a sip of some seriously awful coffee in a plastic cup and was wondering how to dispose of it when the door opened. A woman entered carrying a file and sat down at the desk opposite. *She must be well in her fifties,* he thought. For somebody who was high up in the SFO, you'd think she would look the part. Really, she looked as though she cleaned the offices, not ran them. Then she opened the file, looked at him, and he immediately changed his mind. Her eyes were like a shark's, black and expressionless. This was one tough bitch.

"Well?"

"They were both there, the pair of them. As soon as the body disappeared through the curtains, they went and chatted her up. Since then, she's been to Drage's solicitors and I'm bloody sure she agreed that they handle the probate."

The woman nodded. "She's a hairdresser, isn't she? Makes sense." Her voice was cultured but curt. He nodded. She continued, "Right. Probate shouldn't take too long as she's the only beneficiary. The interesting thing is, who told them she was attending the funeral? From what I read, she wasn't close to her uncle, was she? My gut tells me there's a mole somewhere."

"His solicitors arranged the funeral and cremation. I checked. I assume the mole is there."

"I agree. Keep on it, Greg, and let me know of any developments. Drage died before we had sufficient grounds to arrest him but we need to screw those two bastards into the ground with evidence."

"Yes, ma'am. Is there anything else?"

"Yes. Please remove that plastic cup and its revolting contents from my desk."

September, 2019

Mandy Culverhouse and Rita Sharman had made a rare trip into Stonechester and were sitting in 'Good Days' coffee shop, discussing the latest information received regarding the wold. Rita had caused rather a stir when choosing her drink up at the counter. She had looked at the long list of coffees available and told the nice man serving her that she thought they were very erotic.

"She means exotic," explained Mandy. "Which one do you want, Rita? My treat."

"Er, I'll have a Columbian Cappuccino, please."

"I'll try the Ethiopian. Black for me, please."

"Take a seat, ladies, and I'll bring them over to you." This from a very tall man with a badly scarred face that had creased into a huge grin at Rita's words. Now they were comfortably seated by the window, sipping their brews.

"We really must do something about this, Rita," said Mandy, putting her cup back on its saucer.

"Why? Don't you like your coffee?"

"No, the coffee's fine. I mean about this proposal to build on the wold and all that goes with that. All the Pyddel Valley will end up being built on for road access and all the lovely countryside will disappear. Us walkers must do something to stop it."

"How are we going to do that?" Rita's brow was furrowed with concern. "I read these envelopers have some powerful backers and lawyers and that. What can us lot do?"

Mandy stared through the window at Next's back wall and sighed. Ignoring Rita's verbal faux pas, she replied, "We will object in the strongest possible terms. It will take a lot of effort because we will really need to go to town on this. Mike says there'll have to be a public enquiry anyway, once the planning application goes in. The developers will have to show exactly what their plans are. Things like the access roads, drainage and all that kind of things, and also, how it will affect us, the people. I expect they'll say it will bring jobs to Stonechester and all that sort of thing. Which it will, I suppose, but at what price?"

Rita nodded. "I totally agree with you. I was born and brought up in Middle Piddle. We used to go into Stonechester on the bus to the disco in one of the clubs there on a Saturday night, when I was a teenager. The wold was the place we used to go up to for blackberrying and, in the summer, we used to go swimming in the mere or in the Pyddel itself. It was lovely. Still is, as us walkers know." Mandy nodded.

"It's all about money, not people. I suspect that the labour up here is loads cheaper than down south." Mandy took another sip of her coffee. "But Stonechester is a real dump nowadays. We moved here when I was eight, and there was a lovely market every Wednesday and Saturday.

There were loads of independent shops all along the High Street as well as your Boots, Woolworths and all."

Rita nodded. "It's all gone to seed since Marks & Spencer closed down. There's no reason to come in here nowadays."

Mandy suddenly put down her cup into its saucer and stared hard at Rita. "That's it," she stated. "I'm determined to do my best to prevent all this crap happening. Are you up for it, Rita?"

"I am," she quietly affirmed. "So are loads of others. Len's heard them talking in the pub. There was also a terrific turn out at the first PVP meeting, wasn't there? All we need is lots more people to join us and that means getting the news out in and around Stonechester."

"Internet, here we come." Mandy smiled. "Shall we have another cup of coffee to celebrate?"

***

All the pews in St Agatha's were full for the second PVP meeting. Neither, the Reverend Michael Fuller nor his sister had seen anything like it. It was Sunday afternoon on a lovely autumn day; the setting sun's rays were shining through the stained-glass windows on the west wall of the church, bringing to life again the saints forgiving repentant sinners. The faces in the pews sparkled and twinkled in the rainbow light.

Once again, Lady Caroline Fryers-Faversham was holding forth from the pulpit. Her husband, Brigadier

General (Retired) Sir Henry, was sitting in the front pew looking rather embarrassed if the truth be told.

"So, what is the latest news on this travesty; this proposed destruction of our wonderful English countryside?" she boomed. Mandy Culverhouse stood up and addressed the assembly, "Rita Sharman and myself have tried to do some investigation into the Local Planning Authority but really couldn't get much information from them. However, the impression we got was that something big is really going on. Some company has applied for outline planning permission to build six warehouses and a solar panel farm as well as two access roads. Strangely, though, there's been nothing in the council minutes about all this."

"Well done, ladies," Lady Caroline congratulated them from on high. "I should—"

"Er, sorry, but just one more thing." Mandy cut across, apologetically. Lady Caroline glared at her. Mandy continued, unabashed. "Mike, my husband, works for Coleman, James & Wright in Norbrough. He's got one of his colleagues to do some digging with the land registry and, as we told you at our last meeting, Chris Tilley's land has been bought by what appears to be a shell company and that same company has put in for the outline planning permission. However, as you know, Ted Drage died and his land has been inherited by a niece. All the legal stuff is being handled by Harding, Russell in Stonechester, apparently."

"Oh them lot!" a man called out. "They're a right bunch of crooks, they are!" Everybody looked around at the speaker. He stood up.

"Me name's Tom Healey. I had dealings with them lot when my old mum died. She died intestate and without a will too, and it took well over a year before I got her estate, even though I was her only kid. They ripped me off big time with their fees."

"Yeah, I remember, Tom," called another man from the other side of the church. "They really screwed you, didn't they?"

"Gentlemen," called Lady Caroline, looking more and more like an avenging angel. "Please remember where you are."

"Sorry, love," apologised Tom. "Sorry, Vicar." He nodded in the Reverend Fuller's direction and sat down. The Reverend smiled back in absolution. Mandy stood up again.

"Ladies and gentlemen. I'd like to make a suggestion. We do need to start doing something now. Please, can you spread the word amongst all your family and friends. The more adverse publicity this receives, the better for us all." To her surprise, Rita Sharman found herself standing up beside her friend.

"You all know me and my Len, don't you? Well, one of the *Stonechester Gazette* reporters often comes into our pub, so Len'll prime him about all this and he might be able to do more investigation for us, too. He might have contracts."

"She means contacts," offered Mandy, helpfully. "Meanwhile, I also suggest that us walkers go along the Pyddel Valley and up onto the wold every day, just to check if anything's going on. I also think we should expand our *WhatsApp* group so that we can let everybody know fast if anything happens."

"Oh, please, don't worry about keeping any eye out for trouble," called out Julia Carrington-Herbert. "I'll hack out there, every day, either with my clients or alone, and sound the alert if there's anything amiss."

"My Brian here is often up on the wold, so he'll be keeping an eye out, too. He'll get his fellow twitchers to do the same. Won't you, love." This from Lorraine Ramsbottom. There was a collective nod of agreement from Brian and his fellow birdwatchers.

"That's great, Lorraine. Thank you and you too, Brian." Mandy smiled at everybody.

"What about using social media?" called a man at the back. "You know, *Facebook, Twitter, TikTok* and *Instagram.* We could do a regular blog and then everyone in the world could see it."

"Thank you for that. It's a great idea. Does anyone know how to set it up?" asked Mandy.

"My Kevin's good at that sort of thing." A woman sitting with a group of her friends in one of the side pews stood up. "My name's Lettice Miller, although I'm usually called Letty for short. I belong to the yoga group." She waved her hand at the rest of her pew. "These are my friends who do yoga, too. This is Elizabeth Davis." The lady beside her stood up and waved at the assembly. "Just call me Betty," she informed everyone. Letty continued, "And this is Henrietta Hodson, otherwise known as Hetty." Another woman beside Betty stood up and waved to the audience. Letty had finished the introductions but added, "Yes, my Kevin is in IT so he knows all about computers and all this sort of thing. I'll ring him when I get home." She sat down. Mandy smiled at them all, trying not to laugh. You couldn't make it up: Betty, Hetty and Letty. They sounded like a music hall act.

"I think that's about it from me. Thank you everyone." Mandy sat down.

Barbera stood up. "Well, I think the next step is for me to take your mobile numbers for our *WhatsApp* group, if you haven't already joined it. If you haven't, please could you jot your name and number down on this piece of paper for me." She held out a large sheet of paper and a pen. Everyone stood up and made a beeline towards her or to the tea urn, chattering amongst themselves. Lady Caroline glared down at Mandy but her husband just smiled to himself. Caroline did so hate having her thunder stolen.

***

"So, you're going to be a very rich man, Doug," yawned Sonia Bailey as she stretched out beside him on the king size bed.

"You bet, babe." Douglas Yardley-Henderson smiled, smugly. "If this works out, I'll be a millionaire at least twice over, if not more. I've got the buyers who want to develop the land all lined up. Just need to get Drage's niece to sell up and then we're almost home and dry."

"And what about me? Do I figure in all these millions?" She propped herself up on the pillows and looked down at him.

"Of course, of course." His placating tone annoyed her. Really, he was a right bastard. She often wondered why she had become involved with him. He was married; he was a lousy lover. In fact, it was only the promise of loads of money that kept her with him – in and out of bed. Their trysts were hardly passionate, more of a rut, she thought. No foreplay, no finesse, just fucking. It really was a lie back and think of England, although in her case, it was lying back and thinking about all that money.

"What about Eve? You are going to divorce her and marry me, aren't you?" She sighed inwardly and began to massage his chest and abdomen, each movement moving downwards. He tensed under her touch and she could feel the usual dampness in his groin.

"Of course, of course," he repeated. Then, "Wow, babe, I'm gonna have to make your day."

As Sonia lay back resignedly, she wasn't thinking of England but of New York, the Caribbean, yachts and Greek Islands. It helped.

***

Kevin Miller joined his boyfriend, Steve Barlow, at their favourite table in the Dick vins Dyke Club, Sheep Street, Norbrough, bringing with him two glasses of extremely palatable Australian Merlot. The club founded some five years ago by Mrs Sara Rollins to specifically cater for the LGBTQ+ community in Norssex, offered excellent wines, good food and a haven and solace for its members in a tough, heterosexual world. It was also patronised by 'straights' who also enjoyed the excellent wines and food on offer. It was certainly a huge step up from its Stonechester counterpart, MEN-taur, an on-line dating agency which was known locally as 'Prick and Collect'.

"There you go, Steve. Did you want anything to eat? Sara's revamped the menu, and it looks really appetising."

"Not now, love. I'd just like to enjoy the wine. Perhaps, later." Steve took an appreciative sniff and then a sip. "Lovely. Thank you. Just what the doctor ordered."

Kevin regarded Steve with affection and sympathy. "Rough shift on the ward?" Steve nodded. He was a registrar in Stonechester General's A & E.

"Never mind. Enjoy your wine. Christ knows you deserve it, love."

"What's new with you, Kev?"

"Nothing much really. Just the usual." Kevin sipped his wine and smiled. "Oh yeah, just a bit of minor stuff. Mum phoned me up and asked me to do some private work for her. I say her but it's really for a campaign to stop some developers building roads and warehouses along the Pyddel Valley and up on the wold. Apparently, there are two landowners involved. One has already sold up and the other died, leaving his estate to some niece. Mum wants me to set up a lot of social media accounts, you know like *Facebook*, so that people know what's going on."

Steve grinned. "Well, you might as well add to the Zuckerberg and Microsoft trillions. But that's a real shame, Kev. It's really lovely countryside up there. Dad used to take me fishing along the river, and we used to go blackberrying up on the wold."

"Yeah, I know. I agree with Mum when she said it's rural vandalism. Those warehouses, they've already built at the top of the A6, took ages before anybody moved into them and one is still empty. I reckon it's land speculation and somebody is out to make a packet."

"What's this?" A female voice interrupted their conversation.

"Hi, Sara. Come and join us if you have the time," invited Steve. A tall, slim woman in her forties sat down at their table. She was simply made up and looked elegant in her tailored jeans and cashmere jumper.

"Is the wine OK?" she enquired.

"Really nice, thanks, Sara," said Kevin.

"I've just bought in some new Chilean Cabernet that was highly recommended by two very nice ladies who popped earlier this week, so perhaps, give it a try, next time you come and see if you agree. By the way, Steve, lunch is on the house for you. You look as if you could do with some decent food. I bet you didn't eat anything during your shift." Steve grinned at his admission.

"Thanks a lot," he said. Sara became immediately more business-like.

"So, what's this with the wold, guys? Sorry, but I couldn't help but overhear what you said."

Kevin filled her in. She sat for a moment deep in thought, then looked angry.

"You know, guys, I think this all stinks. I'm local to Stonechester. Mum had me in the general when it was still a small hospital. We lived in a two up, two down in Alexandra Street because Dad was a clicker in one of the shoe factories. But they used to take me out to the wold at weekends. The bus used to run from Stonechester bus station down what is now the A6 to Lower Pyddelham and we used to picnic by the river and climb up the path onto the wold. I can still remember the view. Nowadays, Jo and I take the dogs for a walk up there. Jesus, I can't believe they want to build shitty warehouses on such lovely land! Bastards."

"We both totally agree, Sara, but what can we do?" asked Steve. Sara gave them both a steely glance, her grey eyes glinting.

"Kevin, do what your mum asked," she said, adding, "I'm going to make waves. A lot of people come in here, guys. I'm proud to say this place is very popular with all kinds of people, gays and straights, who work in all sorts of fields, so let me put the word out. I'm bloody sure, we can make a difference."

Kevin and Steve looked at her face. As Kevin remarked later, "Hell hath no fury" sprang to mind.

***

Felicity Holmes re-read the letter from Christiana Morleigh, senior probate manager with Harding, Russell. Uncle Ted's estate was now lodged in her name with the land registry as the 'Grant of Probate' had gone through quite quickly, but then she was the only beneficiary. There were some forms to be signed to allow the solicitors to transfer all monies to her bank account. Felicity decided to deliver the signed forms personally as she wanted to visit the farmhouse and view the land that was now hers. She was also keen to resign from Hair Fair, give up her tiny flat in Edmonton and move abroad, preferably, somewhere sunny and warm. However, she was curious about the farmhouse. As a youngster, she had spent many happy days staying there during the school holidays, helping Aunty Viv in the large kitchen and playing in the sizeable garden. Uncle Ted had been adamant that she shouldn't wander around the farm itself in case of accidents with any of the machinery but, as a treat, he would let her sit beside him on the tractor as it trundled around the fields and across the wold.

She phoned Harding, Russell to arrange an appointment and then booked the day off work. She hadn't told anyone about her 'inheritance' but, with great glee, bought a first class return ticket from St Pancras to Stonechester.

On arrival at the Harding, Russell offices, she was ushered into one of the meeting rooms and was soon joined by a brusque and business-like Christiana Morleigh.

"Good morning, Felicity. I hope you had a good trip here. Tea or coffee?"

"Not for me, thank you. Yes, the train was actually on time." Felicity rummaged in her bag and pulled out the signed documents. "For you."

"Thank you, Felicity. You could have just popped them in the post."

"Yes, I know, but I wanted to come up to look around the farmhouse and the land, if that's OK. It's kind of for old times' sake, I suppose. Here's my bank details for the transfer of monies."

"Thank you, Felicity. I shall pass on this Form of Authority to the Stonechester Building Society, and I'm hopeful you should receive those monies within the next week or so." Christiana smiled at her appraisingly. "You are going to be quite a wealthy lady despite the fact you will have to pay 'inheritance tax'. You see, anything over £325,000 is subject to forty per cent tax. Your uncle's money in the Stonechester Building Society is just over £98,000 and then, of course, you may wish to sell the land, the farmhouse and the outbuildings. All that will bring in a substantial sum."

"Oh yes, I don't think I'd want to keep it."

"I'm absolutely sure, there are investors out there who would be most interested in purchasing it all." Christiana's smile broadened but did not reach her eyes. "Would you like me to pass on your details to these interested parties?"

"Yes, please do, but after I've received the monies into my bank account."

"No problem, Felicity. The Stonechester Building Society will write to you to advise that the transfer of monies has been completed. Meanwhile, would you like one of our conveyancing managers to send you a copy of our 'terms of business' with regard to any sale?"

"That'd be great. Thank you." For some reason, Felicity suddenly felt the need to leave the room. Christiana was really rather intimidating. "Thank you for your help in all of this."

"As soon as everything has been completed, I will be sending you our account for services rendered."

"No, that's fine." Felicity stood up. "I'm going to visit the farmhouse before I return to London, so if you'll excuse me." Christiana stood up. "I'll get Yvonne, our receptionist, to call you a taxi, if you like."

"Thank you, that'd be great." Really, she felt as if she was the solicitor, and Christiana, the very rich client, not the other way around. Thank God, this was the last time she would be in Christiana's presence; really, the woman gave her the willies.

***

"It's me. Felicity has just left. She's going to liquidate the whole estate. She's happy that we handle the sale. Jeremy Fisher is going to do the conveyancing, so no probs there."

"That's great news. It'll get Doug off my back. I owe you."

"Just make sure I get the money, Fred. I've earned it. You owe me big time, for this and the other 'jobs' I've done for you."

"There's no need to be like that."

"Yes, there bloody well is, Fred. Without me, you would never have got this far. Tell that to that fucking twat, Douglas Yardley-Henderson."

"OK, OK. Calm down. You'll get your money."

"You'd better be right, Fred. There's no way I'm going to do probate for the rest of my life. Life's too fucking short."

"I said OK. Calm down and be a bit patient, for Christ's sake. It's all looking good. We just need Felicity to sell the land, and then we're home and dry."

***

Felicity was deep in thought, nestled in the comfortable cushioned seat supplied to travellers in first class. The scenery flitting by, viewed through a rather grubby window, mirrored the speed of her thoughts and the headache, she had acquired in the Cat and Cradle, had almost gone, thanks mainly to a couple of paracetamols.

She had asked the taxi driver to drop her off in Lower Pyddleham, so that she could walk along the road leading up to the farm. It was another beautiful autumn day; sunlight and blue sky was being filtered through a sieve of bronzed leaves. She could hear a thrush singing above her. And all the memories surrounded her like a living cloak. How many times had she walked along this road as a child, chatting happily to Aunty Viv as they made their way to the farmhouse, stopping occasionally to pick the blackberries from the hedgerows sentried along their path. Christ, they were good days.

The first thing Felicity noticed was that the gate leading to the farmhouse was badly in need of repair; twisted and rusted, it was obvious it hadn't seen a lick of paint in years. She was able to squeeze through a gap between it and the overgrown hedge. Approaching the farmhouse itself, she could see it had been badly neglected, as had the buildings dotted around it. Peeping inside the biggest one, she saw the old tractor again. Uncle Ted used to let her ride on it. The next building was the one in which Henry, the cob, used to live. His stall was empty but the old tack – cobwebbed together, was still hanging from hooks on the wall. The memory of sitting on Henry for the first time returned to her vividly. How excited she had been. How proud!

The farmhouse beckoned. She tried the front door and wasn't surprised to find it locked but a gentle shove against the jamb easily broke the latch. Entering the hallway disturbed the drifts of dust and cobwebs. The smell was awful: damp, decay, death, but she continued through to the kitchen, where she had spent so many happy hours with her aunt, through to the living room and then up the stairs to the bedrooms and bathroom. She ignored the latter but walked through the three bedrooms, looking out of the windows. What wonderful views! The Pyddel was twinkling back at her from its valley with the villages of Lower and Middle Pyddelham visible in the autumn aura. She could also make out the new housing of Upper Pyddelham as the river curved upstream towards Stonechester and, in the far distance, a glint of traffic on the A14 as it wound its polluted way to the south of the town.

From her old bedroom window at the back of the farmhouse, she traced the rise of the land as it fused with the wold and caught a glimpse of the mere where she had fished for sticklebacks with one of Aunty Viv's stockings on a bamboo stick and a jar that had once contained Aunty Viv's homemade blackberry jam.

Sighing, she returned downstairs, saddened by her memories and the neglect of the whole place; the emotion deepened when she saw the garden, or what remained of it. The old vegetable beds were now hidden under weeds and brambles. The roses had certainly rambled, their petals caught among the black spotted, curled, aphid eaten leaves. Aunty Viv's flower bed was a mass of weeds, choking the light away from the penstemons, dahlias and the other perennials that were so colourful during the summer. As for the apple and pear trees, Felicity stood looking at the twisted, broken and diseased trunks like a mourner by the side of a newly dug grave.

After some time, she walked around to the front door and pulled it upright to give the appearance that it was locked. She then made her way back down the path towards Lower Pyddelham. So deep in thought, she didn't realise that she was being hailed by a man, dressed in khaki fatigues with binoculars around his neck.

"Hallo there," he said. "Are you lost?"

"No, I'm not." She went to walk away but he followed her. She began to feel panicky. Was he going to attack her? Rape her? She began to run.

"Please stop, me duck," he called. "I mean you no harm. Honest. It's just I was doing my birdwatching and I saw you come down from Ted Drage's place. Me name's Brian, Brian Ramsbottom."

Felicity slowed down and looked at him. He had a nice face. Besides which, his name was familiar.

"Are you the Brian who married Lorraine Lucas?"

"That's me, all right. We've been married nearly twenty-eight years now. Who are you then, if you remember my Lorraine?"

"I'm Felicity Holmes. Ted Drage was my uncle, although my Aunty Viv was my mum's sister."

"Oh, right. I was sorry to hear about Ted." Felicity had now reduced her run to a ramble pace. She and Brian were now walking together down the road back to Lower Pyddelham.

"Are you going to sell up then?" Brian had no idea of subtlety, only curiosity.

"Yes, I am." They had stopped by St Agatha's church. "I went up there to sort of say goodbye. The whole place is a real mess. It's such a shame really. I've got some lovely memories. You know, when I was a kiddie and I used to come and stay with Uncle Ted and Aunty Viv." Brian patted her kindly on the arm.

"Yeah, I know. Nothing ever stays the same, does it?" Then remembering he had to report this turn of events back to his wife and everyone else, he continued. "So, it's all going through, is it?" Felicity nodded.

"Yes. The probate's come through and I've instructed Harding, Russell to handle the sale of Uncle Ted's land and buildings."

"Right, right." Brian nodded, sagely. "Well, you know they probably want to build warehouses on it and a bloody great road, too?"

"No, I didn't actually. Look, that's a real shame but I don't want it. I'm not a farmer, am I. I'm a hairdresser and I just want to settle it all and go and live my life." Felicity's words tumbled out of her; the emotions of the day were taking their toll. Besides which Brian was such a nice bloke.

Brian patted her arm, again. "Look, love. Let me buy you a drink at the Cat and Cradle. You look a bit peaky, actually. I'll call Lorraine and ask her to join us, so you know it's all kosher and that I'm not a white slaver or nothing."

Felicity grinned at him. Brian looked just what he was: a middle-aged, balding birdwatcher. He directed her to a rather well used, muddy Fiesta, and they both drove to the Cat and Cradle in Upper Pyddelham.

A man sitting in a grey BMW started its engine and, after a minute or so, drove off in the same direction.

***

Lorraine Ramsbottom was already sitting in the snug nursing a gin and tonic when Felicity and Brian arrived.

Rita Sharman was helping Len behind the bar but came over as soon as they were seated with Lorraine.

"What can I get you two?"

"Ooh, a rum and coke would be nice." Felicity felt in need of some alcoholic assistance after the past few hours. "Can you put some ice in, please."

"No probs, me duck" – turning to Brian – "a pint of Red Devil, Bri?"

"Please, Rita. And come and join us." Rita nodded and disappeared behind the bar. The Cat and Cradle was quiet now after the lunchtime rush. Just a couple of people in the saloon and another man who had walked into the snug and ordered a pint of Carlsberg. He sat in the inglenook and began reading *The Daily Telegraph.*

Rita returned with the drinks and Len, and they pulled up a couple of stools to join Felicity and the Ramsbottoms.

"This is Felicity Holmes, everyone. She's Ted Drage's niece. I saw her up on the wold earlier, coming from the direction of Ted's place. Felicity, this is my Lorraine." He nodded in her direction. "And this is Len and Rita Sharman who own this pub."

"I'm very pleased to meet you all." Felicity smiled.

"We're very pleased to meet you, too," said Rita. "We've been wondering who was going to be the benefit."

"She means beneficiary," Lorraine chimed in helpfully. "Ted tended to keep himself to himself." They nodded. Felicity took a large sip of her drink.

"I have to tell you that I've decided to put everything up for sale, as I explained to Brian here." Felicity could feel herself relax as the rum kicked in. In fact, there seemed to be more rum than coke.

"No, love, we all do understand, don't we?" This was from Lorraine. They nodded again. She continued, "It's just that we've heard that somebody wants to build warehouses on it and a big access road off the A6. That means that the road will go along the Pyddel Valley, through what was Chris Tilley's land and through your land and onto the wold. If that happens, it'll be a great shame because it's such a lovely part of the countryside."

"I sher your concern, honesh I do." A mixture of rum and guilt was making Felicity slur her words slightly. "But I'm no farmer. I'm a dresser hair." Lorraine patted her hand.

"Let's just hope whoever buys it wants it for farming," she said, hopefully. There was silence, then from the Saloon, "Oi, Len, are you running a dry bar or what?"

"Coming, coming." Len stood up and went to get a drink for the thirsty customer. Felicity was now feeling pleasantly drowsy.

"You said Harding, Russell were handling the sale," Brian stated. She nodded.

"Do you do coffee, Rita? I think this cum and roke has gone straight to my head."

"Certainly. I'll get you an espresso. That'll wake you up."

It had certainly done that, leaving her with a dull ache in her forehead and looking like a bushbaby caught in a searchlight. Rita had given her a couple of paracetamols and a lift to Stonechester railway station – after charging her a substantial sum for everybody's drinks as well as her own. After all, as Len said, business was business; the Cat and Cradle wasn't a charity.

***

Arriving at St Pancras, Felicity took a taxi home. On the way, she decided that she would never ever go to Stonechester again. She was definitely going to sell Uncle Ted's land and wouldn't give a shit if somebody built a nuclear power station on it.

Meanwhile, the man who had been reading *The Daily Telegraph* had enjoyed his Carlsberg and, even more, the conversation that had taken place in the snug. He could now report back to 'super bitch' at the Serious Fraud Office. He knew she would be pleased with this latest information, but he made a mental note not to take any coffee into her office.

***

"Hi, Mandy, it's me, Rita. Got some really good news for you." Rita cradled her mobile between her ear and shoulder whilst she sliced up some carrots.

"Hiya! What's been happening?" Mandy perched herself on one of the stools around the kitchen island and put Rita on her mobile's loudspeaker whilst she poured herself a glass of chardonnay. She didn't interrupt Rita's flow until Rita had drawn breath.

"Right, well, well done to Brian and Lorraine and, of course, you and Len. It was a real piece of luck Brian saw her up there."

"Oh, Brian's been going up onto the wold almost daily according to Lorraine. Either on his own or with some of his twitchers. He's really worried that any development up there will scare off all the birds. All the birdwatchers are, apparently."

"What about us walkers, Rita? The wold and the Pyddel Valley are valued by us, too. As I told you previously, I'm bloody determined to get any warehousing stopped."

"Mandy, what can we do then? That Felicity is determined to sell up. To be fair, I can understand why, but if she sells out to these enveloper people, we're stuffed."

"Well, according to Mike, they would have to get planning permission, first of all, from the local authority. In our case, it's going to be Stonechester Borough Council. Also something like this has to go out to public consultation before any such permission is granted, so if everyone kicks up about it, we should get it stopped."

"That'd be good, Mandy. But the thing is, if somebody buys the land, they'll want to do something with it, don't they?"

"Then let's hope, it might be another farmer or someone. At least, someone who doesn't want to build a load of bloody warehouses. I think it's time for another meeting of the PVP. I'll send a round robin on our *WhatsApp* group so everybody knows the latest."

"That's great. By the way, Mandy. Do you know if Kevin Miller's done all the social medium side like his mum said?" Mandy ignored her faux pas.

"Good question, Rita. I'll text Letty Miller and find out. Anything else?"

"No, that's about it. Interesting, though, that Harding, Russell is involved yet again. You know, Mandy, I've got a gut feeling that there's something not right in all of this. It stinks."

"Oh, bet your life that somebody's going to make an absolute packet if this all goes through. There's somebody on the take, probably someone on the council, I reckon."

"I'll let you know if Len or me hear anything in the pub."

"Thanks, Rita, and thanks for the call. See you soon."

After Rita had said her goodbyes, Mandy continued sitting at the kitchen island deep in thought. Rita was absolutely right; the whole thing did stink – to high heaven.

October, 2019

St Agatha's was buzzing. Every pew was full of people chatting to each other in anticipation and expectation. Among some new 'joiners' were Terry Bailey, one of the two *Stonechester Gazette* reporters, and Kevin Miller and Sara Rollins. Steve Barlow couldn't make it; he was working a shift in Stonechester General's A & E. Another new joiner, an innocuous looking woman, sat right at the back, almost hidden by the organ pipes. She regarded the proceedings with great interest, her ink black eyes unblinking.

Lady Caroline Fryers-Faversham mounted the pulpit; the Reverend Michael Fuller winced as the seventeenth century oak wood construction groaned under her weight.

"Can I have your attention everyone," she boomed. Immediately, the church became silent. She continued, "Thank you all for coming here today for a meeting of the PVP. As you will know, there have been developments since we last met, and I will now ask Mrs Amanda Culverhouse to bring this meeting up to speed. Mrs Culverhouse." She nodded graciously in Mandy's direction.

Mandy stood up and nodded back. "Thank you, Lady Caroline." She faced the congregation. "Well, you all know the latest by now, courtesy of Mr Kevin Miller.

Thanks, Kevin, for doing all the social media work for us, by the way. You can find us on *Twitter, Instagram, Facebook, TikTok.* I'd also like to welcome Terry Bailey from the *Stonechester Gazette.* Terry?"

Terry Bailey stood up and waved. He sat down again and began writing in his notebook. Mandy continued, "Ted Drage's land is going up for sale, just like Chris Tilley's was. I suspect the same people, who bought Chris's, will try and buy Ted's. That would make good financial sense." There was absolute silence; she had her audience's total attention.

"The problem is, what are these purchasers going to do with all that land, the land that many of us have known from childhood, the land that many of us still enjoy? What will happen to the Pyddel Valley or, indeed, the river itself?" She sighed. "Well, it appears that it could all well disappear under warehouses, a solar panel farm and major road access from the A6. The question is: do we need any more warehousing? Only five of the six warehouses built to the north of Stonechester are occupied, and they were completed nearly three years ago." She shrugged. "It's not as if there are loads of unemployed people in this area either."

There was a collective murmur of assent at her words. "I'm going to have to be careful here," she continued. "Because of charges of slander but the same names keep cropping up in all of this which" – she gazed around the assembly – "makes me think that somebody is going to make an absolute packet if all this warehousing, solar and whatnot – plus the road thing – goes through."

The silence was absolute. Then a woman's voice asked, "So who do you think is involved? Without naming names."

"It's got to be somebody on the Stonechester Borough Council and/or Norssex County Council," a man's voice called out. "You don't have to be Sherlock bloody Holmes to work that one out."

"Please," boomed Lady Caroline from her liturgical perch. "There's no need to swear."

"I agree totally," said Mandy and many of the congregation nodded. "I think we have to do some digging – if you'll pardon the pun." Many smiled but everyone was looking very determined. Their forefathers, who had put a Roman legion and the marauding Danes to shame, would be proud.

Terry Bailey stood up. Heads swivelled in his direction. He said, "Just let me know if I can help you with getting all that sort of intel together. Like Mrs Culverhouse said, we do have to be careful in naming people in case we get done for libel and slander. We'll need proper proof and the *Stonechester Gazette* will be proud to play its part in bringing any, er, malpractice into the public domain."

"Thanks a lot, Mr Bailey. We will certainly keep you and your newspaper in the loop." Mandy smiled in his direction as he sat down. "OK, are there any questions or comments?" There were some murmurings. Then the lady with the black eyes sitting at the back put her hand up. Heads that were able to do so, swivelled once again, this time in her direction.

"Has anybody been checking the meeting minutes of both councils?"

Mandy nodded. "Yes, we have but there's been nothing about warehousing on the wold or access roads. However, I shall keep checking each time the minutes come out. The Land Registry is also regularly checked. That's how we found out about the Tilley land being sold to this shell company, DAYH Investments." The lady with the black eyes nodded.

"Anyone else?" Mandy asked. There was silence again but it was the hopeful silence of expectation, in this case free tea, coffee and biscuits.

"Thanks, everyone. Please keep in touch via our *WhatsApp* group and keep an eye on our *Facebook, Instagram* etc. accounts." Mandy sat down. Lady Caroline noted that the two large urns' lids were rattling from the steam.

"Tea up, everyone," she called as she made her way heavily down the pulpit stairs. There was a mass exodus from the pews and a babble of talk. The lady with the ink black eyes slipped out of St Agatha's, a satisfied smile on her thin lips.

November, 2019

"Guess what, babe!" Douglas Yardley-Henderson was exultant. He and Sonia had just walked into a hotel room in London after attending a conference about investments in the Pacific Rim countries called 'Your Money, Your Reward, Your World'.

"Just had a call from the Stonechester Conservative Club. They want to put me forwards as their next candidate for the seat since old Lloyd wants to spend more time with his family or so they said. Anyhow, babe, you could be looking at the next Conservative MP for Stonechester very shortly. You lucky, lucky lady!"

As he pushed her onto the bed, still fully dressed, and began pulling at her underwear, she thought that it should be conservative with a very small "c" and that, right now, she should be singing 'Land of Grope and Tory'.

***

"Miss Holmes? Good morning, it's Christiana Morleigh, Harding, Russell."

"Oh, good morning." Felicity stopped uncurling her 11:00 a.m. perm and removed her mobile from between her ear and shoulder. "One moment, please." She looked at the woman in the mirror and hissed, "Sorry, got to take this call."

"OK, can you talk?"

"Yes, please, go ahead."

"I'm very pleased to say that your late uncle's estate has passed probate, and as you are the sole beneficiary, the land and his financial assets are now yours. Please accept my congratulations."

"Oh, that's fantastic. Thank you."

"I shall, of course, be writing to you to confirm all of this. The Stonechester Building Society has been notified and they will be sending you a cheque to your home address shortly."

"Oh, wow!" Felicity's voice was breathless. *At long bloody last,* she thought.

"Yes, indeed. I will, of course, also be including our fees for our work on your late uncle's estate, probate, etc., and we would be most pleased if you would settle it as soon as possible."

"Yes, of course I will."

"Thank you. Just one other matter." Christiana's voice tailed off from her brusque business-like manner to more of a silky caress. It made Felicity feel uncomfortable.

"Your late uncle's land and buildings. Do you still wish to sell it?"

"Oh, yes. I've no interest in it at all."

"Well, I do know somebody who would be very interested in it. Would you like Harding, Russell to act as intermediaries? Our conveyancing department would be delighted to act for you. Jeremy Fisher, our conveyancing compliance manager and licensed conveyancer, would be your contact if you decide to go ahead. Obviously, there will be our fees involved."

Obviously, thought Felicity. She took a deep breath.

"No, no. That's all fine. Please contact your interested party and say I want to sell. I want to sell as soon as possible."

"Thank you, Miss Holmes. I will go ahead as you have instructed and confirm all this in writing. Is there anything else we can do for you?"

Felicity had the sudden mad urge to ask Christiana to finish off her 11:00 a.m. perm but restrained herself.

"No, no, I think that's it for now."

Christiana's voice returned to its usual brusque tone.

"If you think of anything else, please don't hesitate to contact me. Goodbye, Miss Holmes."

Felicity switched off her mobile, put it in her pocket and returned to uncurling the 11:00 a.m. perm who was now looking daggers at her through the mirror. Her emotions were a maelstrom of elation, relief and excitement. She could make plans for a new life now. Although, she wanted to walk out there and then leave her old life behind, she decided that as soon as she received the cheque, she'd resign and then tell her landlord what he could do with his shitty, little over-priced flat.

***

"Fred, it's me. The probate's through and she wants to sell as soon as possible. She's happy for Russell, Harding to act on her behalf. I'll be briefing Jeremy Fisher."

"Thank Christ for that. Does she know much about land prices?"

"She knows sweet FA, so you should be able to pick it up fairly cheaply; she's no Chris Tilley."

"Great. I'll let Doug know. He's got the developers on his back. They want us to put in for outline planning permission."

"That might take time since it's agricultural land, and there should be an agricultural holding number issued by Defra. Did Ted Drage have anything like that? There's a load of regulations about using what was agricultural land for commercial purposes but then you'd know about that, Fred. Wouldn't you? In your capacity as Norssex county councillor and leader of Stonechester Borough Council?"

He ignored her question. "Thanks for letting me know, Christiana. Doug and me will put together an offer for her."

"I'll leave it with you. But, Fred, you screw me over on my cut of the deal and I'll…"

"Don't worry, Christiana. You'll get your money."

"I'm not worrying, Fred. I'll let you do that."

December, 2019

Eve Yardley-Henderson was living a most enjoyable life. The daughter of a minor viscount, she had brought to her marriage an excellent blood line, a well-respected family name, a bevy of contacts, both political and aristocratic that read straight from Debrett's, and her own shrewd, streetwise eye for the main chance.

She had had no illusions about Douglas when she agreed to marry him. She knew he had only married her to further his own career and she, in her way, admired him for that. It was truly a symbiotic relationship. However, as time went on, despite all the trappings of affluence, she had begun to despise him because of his inept attempts to persuade her he was faithful.

Quite quickly after their marriage, she had realised there were more than two of them in it. This she accepted – as long as she could continue to live the life she aspired to: Caribbean cruises, shopping trips to Paris and New York, entertaining the great and the good and a cabinet minister or two in their mock Tudor six bedroomed 'lodge' in Lower Pyddelham and organising drinks and amuses bouchées post the Norssex Hunt. She was the archetypal chess player; her husband, friends and acquaintances were manoeuvred around the chessboard of their shared lives with deft, quick moves without them even realising they were merely pawns in Eve's get power game.

So it was that on this particular Wednesday morning, as she lay back on the couch for her weekly facial, the crisp, snow-white towels enfolding her in a soft, aromatic caress, she felt very pleased with life; Doug was now the prospective Conservative MP candidate for Stonechester. All her networking, meetings, entertaining and, well, brown-nosing, but she nimbly pushed that thought away, had at last come to fruition. As Antonia switched on the whale song CD and began to massage her forehead, Eve breathed into her dream of a permanent life in London and, perhaps, even a home in Downing Street, although she would certainly change the décor that Boris and Carrie had chosen. Some people had no taste at all. She smiled to herself. Life really was quite lovely.

***

Edna Denton lived very quietly. She gardened quietly; she knitted quietly; she cooked and cleaned quietly. She was a quiet person, almost to the point of being invisible. She didn't have any friends, only nodding acquaintances met during the Norssex and Stonechester councils' functions, which she quietly attended whenever Fred told her to. She blended into the background, camouflaged by the veneers of middle-class living and respectability. But she also observed and listened. Very quietly!

***

Another meeting of the PVP was taking place at St Agatha's. This time it was standing room only. Reverend Michael Fuller was ecstatic at the turnout and his sister, Barbera, had had to purchase another tea urn to cater for the increase in numbers. Now three urns stood on a table just below the pulpit, their lids playing a tympanic chorale as the steam lifted them into the air, threatening to make the ginger nuts and digestives go soggy and melt the chocolate on the Jaffa cakes.

Lady Caroline Fryers-Faversham was absent today. Her husband, Sir Henry, had given Lady Caroline's apologies to both Mandy Culverhouse and Rita Sharman, explaining that she had mis-timed a shot on the twelfth hole green at Norbrough Golf Club, had fallen over her no. 2 iron and hurt her back. Both ladies asked him to pass on their good wishes for a speedy recovery. Sir Henry, looking unusually chirpy, now sat in the front pew chatting to an attractive, athletic lady from the Stonechester Yoga and Keep Fit Group.

"Go on, Mandy," said Rita. "You're in charge today."

"No, I'm not, Rita. This is a group effort. We're all in this together."

"Well, you'd better start it off then." Rita gave Mandy a gentle push towards the pulpit. Mandy reluctantly climbed the stairs; the Reverend Michael Fuller was relieved to see that Mandy was much slimmer and lighter than Lady Caroline and that the pulpit did not object.

"Er, ladies and gentlemen, please, can I have your attention," Mandy called out. Immediately, the chatter died down and everyone looked up at her expectantly. She gulped, not used to all this attention.

Bugger this for a game of soldiers, she thought. *I feel like a bloody moving target standing up here.*

She descended the pulpit stairs and stood in the middle aisle.

"First of all, thank you all for coming to this meeting of the PVP. Your support is really appreciated. Secondly, I'd like to bring you all up to speed with the latest news." She took a deep breath and continued, "Ted Drage's land is being put up for sale." There was dead silence, then, "How d'you know that?" called a voice.

"My husband works for a firm of solicitors in Norbrough and one of his colleagues told him that the land registry has shown a change of ownership. The new owner is, as we all thought, Ted's niece. I'm pretty sure, she won't want to farm it."

"I can confirm she won't." Rita stood up beside Mandy. "I met her, along with Lorraine and Brian here, way back in September." She nodded over towards them and they both stood up. Brian started to speak but Lorraine cut across him.

"Brian met Ted's niece up on the wold and brought her back to the Cat and Cradle. She told us and Rita and Len that she wanted to sell up. She said she's got no interest in farming the land or keeping it. She just wants the money as quickly as possible. That's what she told us."

"Does anyone know who the buyers are then?" called the same voice.

"Not yet but you can be sure it'll be the company that bought out Chris Tilley," Mandy answered. "That'd make complete business sense as I said at the last meeting." Everyone was nodding sagely, and there was a Mexican wave of murmuring in the pews. "I bet Harding, Russell are handling all the legal stuff," called out Tom Healey from one of the middle pews.

"Why do you say that?" called another man, who had been sitting quietly in a pew right at the back.

"Cos they're the biggest firm of solicitors in Stonechester and cos they're a bunch of thieves," Tom replied.

"I think you're probably right, Ted. I dare say we'll soon find out. I'll ask my husband if he can check it out. Thanks for that." Mandy smiled at him. "Before we close this meeting, there's just one other development. In the latest Stonechester Borough Council minutes, under 'any other business', there was a reference made for a proposed new 'access road' to be discussed at the next meeting. That was all. It didn't say where this road was planned to go. I'll make sure I read the next minutes as soon as they come out, and that'll be in January. We'll have another PVP meeting then. Thank you all so much for listening. Would anyone like to say or add anything?"

Reverend Michael Fuller put up his hand. "May I say a few words?"

"Of course, Reverend." Mandy sat down beside Rita with a sigh of relief. She was pleased to be out of the spotlight. The Reverend came and stood in front of the altar steps.

"Ladies and gentlemen, before we break for refreshments, I'd just like to let you know about the Christmas festivities planned for St Agatha's. My sister, Barbera, has kindly compiled a list, and we both hope you will all continue to come to this church to enjoy them. You will find them beside the ginger nuts. We have endeavoured to offer something for all ages but everyone is welcome. Now, do please help yourselves to the refreshments."

There was a babble of conversation and a collective rush towards the tea urns, now under the firm control of Barbera Fuller and two of her stalwart church wardens. Mandy looked at Rita.

"Rita, sod tea and coffee. I could murder a G and T."

Rita grinned understandingly.

"Follow me, young Amanda. Tanqueray, Fever Tree and the snug await you," Mandy grinned back.

"You're a good mate, Rita. Lead on, Macduff."

"Who's Macduff?"

***

Felicity Holmes was leafing through some long-haul holiday brochures during her lunch break when Jeremy Fisher rang her. She had agreed to work a month's notice and had also given notice to her landlord. A near six figure cheque had been deposited in her bank account; the amount decreased by the Harding, Russell fees. Felicity had been quite shocked at their charges but had been happy to reimburse them, no questions asked, just to obtain closure.

"Good afternoon, Miss Holmes." Jeremy had a very soft, cultured voice, almost soothing. How different from Christiana Morleigh's brusque tones. "Is it convenient to speak."

"Oh, no probs. Please, go ahead."

"With regard to the purchase of your land and buildings located outside Stonechester, I have received an offer from the interested parties concerned. They are offering £8,000 an acre. Since your landholding comprises seventy-four acres or thirty hectares, their offer amounts to £592,000. There are, however, some buildings, I believe. A small farmhouse and four outbuildings but none of them appear to be in good repair so there is an additional offer of £80,000. The offer in total, therefore, is £672,000 but the interested party is happy to cover your fees incurred in any sale to them." Jeremy's voice purred. "Would you think of me presumptuous if I were to try and gauge your thoughts, thus far?"

"Er, well, it sounds a good offer, I have to say." Felicity's heart was beating rapidly with excitement but she tried to sound nonchalant. She was tempted to say she would think about it, but there was nothing to think about. Taking a deep breath, she replied, "I accept their offer, Mr Fisher. Please go ahead with the sale." On the other end of the line, Jeremy Fisher was smiling from ear to ear; he looked like his Beatrix Potter alter ego.

"Thank you, Miss Holmes. Harding, Russell will begin the sale process immediately, and I will confirm our discussion today in writing. I will undertake to keep you informed of every development as it happens. Meanwhile, may I offer you the compliments of the season."

"Thank you, Mr Fisher, and a Merry Christmas to you, too."

***

"She's agreed to the selling price, Doug!" Fred Denton sounded, for once, really delighted. "£672,000 all up and Jeremy will waive any fees he can on her side and we've agreed to pick up anything else."

"Fucking brilliant, Fred, and about bloody time, too. The land and the buildings are worth around two million smackers, so we're quids in." Douglas Yardley-Henderson was ecstatic and not a little relieved. His backers were living up to their name; they were on his back.

"Doug, just one thing. Well, two, actually. The first is my 'mole'. She wants her money and so will her conveyancer guy."

"They'll have to bloody wait."

"I'm worried about her, Doug. She can turn really nasty."

"Fred, you really are a gutless wonder. If she threatens to take us down, she'll end up doing stir too. She's as bent as a corkscrew, that one." Douglas sighed. "OK, Fred, give them £10,000 each to be going on with but tell them both from me that that'll be it until the developers sign on the dotted line and that will be after any outline planning permission is granted."

"That brings me to something else that's worrying me, Doug. Apparently, it's got out that Chris's and Ted's land has been sold for development. It's on social media and the locals have got together to form a protest group. The Wellbeing Walkers, or what have you, started it and have got other local groups involved, too."

"Yeah, yeah, Fred. I heard. Eve mentioned something about them. She heard it in her Pilates class or something. Take no notice. It's all smoke and no fire."

"Well in January's council meeting, we have to discuss the proposed access road and then it will have to be formally documented that the wold and adjoining land are up for development."

"So be it, Fred. It had to go public sooner or later. Meanwhile, I don't know about you, but I'm going to have a wonderful Christmas, and 2020 is going to be effing bloody marvellous. Now piss off."

Douglas switched his mobile off and turned to Sonia laying in the queen size bed beside him.

"Well, babe, let's celebrate in the best way we know. To paraphrase Del Boy, this time next year, I'll be a millionaire!"

"Clever boy," she crooned as she climbed on top of him. "Clever boy. Just remember to divorce Eve first otherwise she'll get half."

"Oh yeah. That's right. I'll speak to my solicitor tomorrow."

"Make sure you do, Doug, because this time next year, I'd like to be Mrs Yardley-Henderson."

***

"Doesn't look too good, does it," Lorraine Ramsbottom remarked to Brian after the ten o'clock news had finished.

"What doesn't look too good? Sorry, love, I dozed off."

"This disease that's started in China. It's spreading like mad and it's killing loads of people."

"I wouldn't worry, love. Nothing'll come of it." Brian gave Lorraine a kiss and stood up.

"Coming up to bed?"

"You go up, Brian. I want to finish off a bit of ironing." He disappeared up the stairs. Lorraine got out the ironing board and switched the iron on. As she waited for it to heat up, she couldn't help feeling that this Covid thing was something that should not be ignored.

***

"So where are we, Greg?" Back at the Serious Fraud Office in Cockspur Street, London, the woman with the ink black eyes glanced up at him as he sat down. He always found her stare intimidating and was annoyed at his reaction. Her desk was between them, case notes set out in neat piles, pens and pencils aligned and her computer set in screen saver.

He tried to make himself relax before replying. "The PVP lot are really doing their homework. They've discovered that Felicity Holmes has put Drage's land up for sale with the strong probability that Harding, Russell is acting as a go-between. They've also picked up that an access road is due to be discussed at the Stonechester Borough Council meeting, next month."

She nodded and quickly jotted a few notes in the file open in front of her.

"Anything else?"

"Yes. Miss Holmes has received and banked a cheque from the Stonechester Building Society in the sum of £98,326.21. This was the monies from Ted Drage's account with them. She immediately arranged a bank transfer in the sum of £15,066.45 to Harding, Russell's account with the ROT Bank."

"Quite a substantial sum," she observed. "For a firm of small-town solicitors, they charge London fees." Greg nodded.

"What news of the land sale? Has Miss Holmes been approached directly by Messrs Denton and Yardley-Henderson?"

"No, they haven't. One assumes they're going through Harding, Russell and using the same shell company used for purchasing the Tilley land."

"Right. Do we know the name of the person who'll be doing the conveyancing etc?"

"It's probably a guy called Jeremy Fisher. He's been with Harding, Russell for some years and is their conveyancing compliance manager. I got chatting to the Harding,

Russell receptionist, and she told me that he and Christiana Morleigh are as thick as thieves and that she occasionally receives calls from Fred Denton and a couple from Douglas Yardley-Henderson." Greg thought back to his encounter with Yvonne, the receptionist. He had followed her to a wine bar after work and began chatting her up for information, aided and abetted by numerous glasses of vodka and lime. They had ended up in her tiny bedsit where the inevitable had taken place and the pillow talk afterwards proved to be very interesting. Greg smiled to himself. All in the line of duty and there were some perks to the job. He continued, "Nobody likes either of them, according to the receptionist. She's quite friendly with a couple of the secretaries. She said one of them reckoned there'd been some dodgy dealings both in the past and currently with these two."

"That bloody figures. Right. Well done, Greg. What's the name of the shell company?"

"DAYH Investments. It's registered in the Caymen Islands."

"Well, well, well. The same shell company that bought the Tilley land. Douglas Alexander Yardley-Henderson. The ego of the man – he can't even give a shell company a decent name or use another shell company to buy the Drage land. He's making life very easy for us." She gave a small smile. "Keep on it, Greg. I want to nail this bastard and the other three as well. As soon as the land registry shows a change in ownership, let me know."

"What about Felicity Holmes? Do you want to sequester her bank account?"

"No, we have no proof that Ted Drage's money was acquired from ill-gotten gains, although I'm bloody sure it was. Not yet. She's small fry. I want to go after the sharks first."

January, 2020

The Wellbeing Walkers were taking the opportunity of a chilly, crisp but sunny morning to ramble along the Pyddel Valley and up onto the wold. Well wrapped against the cold breeze, they continued along the hedgerows until the ground fell away and the Pyddel Valley was laid out below them like a living tapestry. The winter sun, low on the horizon at this time of year, picked out the three villages, the steeple of St Agatha's being especially prominent. In the distance, vehicles were rushing along the A14 as if being chased by the devil himself. Red Kites wheeled in ever decreasing circles and called sadly to each other in the bleached blue sky while, nearer to earth, occasional birdsong could be heard.

"It really is lovely up here," remarked Mandy Culverhouse to Rita Sharman. Rita nodded.

"Yes, it's quite magical. Mind, it's always had that sort of feeling. It's truly worth fighting for." Mandy looked at her friend with raised eyebrows. It was rare for Rita to philosophise.

"What are you two in a huddle over?" This from Lorraine Ramsbottom. She came over to join them, accompanied by a couple of the other Wellbeing Walkers.

"Look at the view. Just look at the view," said Rita, pointing out across the valley and then sweeping her arm towards the wold behind them. She sounded like a pigeon cooing. "This is what we're going to save from roads and warehouses and polar farms. How can they think about building on such wonderful land? How dare they!"

Everyone regarded Rita with amazement. Mandy wondered if she'd had a couple of large brandies before coming out this morning. Rita turned around and regarded them all, her soft brown eyes alive with indignation and anger.

"Don't look at me as if I was mad. I was born here. Look, just over there, in Middle Piddle. My family goes back generations there. They farmed all this area for donkey's years. I got wonderful memories, and I'm bloody furious that some greedy bustard wants to build all over it."

Mandy added helpfully, "She means bastard."

"I know what I mean, Mandy! Don't keep bloody connecting me!"

"Sorry, Rita." Mandy tried to sound placating, but she was truly shocked at Rita's behaviour and forgot to say 'correcting'. "I really do apologise, love. Sorry."

Rita appeared to calm down. All the Wellbeing Walkers were staring at her. Nobody had ever seen the quiet, unassuming, spooneristic Rita Sharman so angry before. With as much aplomb as she could muster, Rita nodded.

"OK," she said. "But I'm determined to get this all stopped. This isn't just for us, it's for our children and grandchildren." Then after a few seconds. "And their children."

"Hear, hear, Rita. Well said." This came from a couple of ladies at the back. Mandy nodded, as did the rest of the walkers.

"Yes, you're right, Rita," she said. Turning towards the wold and then back to the Pyddel Valley and the land beyond, she repeated, "Yes, you're absolutely right, Rita. All this is worth fighting for."

***

At the Dick vins Dyke Club in Norbrough, Sara Rollins was deep in thought. She was naturally intuitive and the news that this Covid disease, currently spreading like wildfire, was causing her great concern. Jo, her partner, had told her not to worry; it would turn out to be like SARS in 2004 – a very limited spread. Jo was the headmistress of a Stonechester Infants and Junior School and was presently taken up with an Ofsted inspection. But Sara had always relied on her sixth sense. It had never let her down. Ever. So, when she read about Covid and watched the TV news programmes, she knew instinctively that their lives were going to change radically. For some reason, Steve Barlow working in A & E popped into her mind, together with some others of her clientele who worked either at Norbrough or Stonechester general hospitals.

Meanwhile, even though it was mid-January, the club was doing very well. Business was good and she was considering whether to take on another part-timer. But she couldn't shake off this feeling of impending doom. To try and cheer herself up, she started leafing through some holiday brochures. It was about time she and Jo got away for a lovely holiday. Easter would be a good.

February, 2020

"Jeremy, it's me. How's the Holmes land sale going?" Christiana Morleigh had closed her office door and contacted him mobile to mobile.

"Can't speak at the moment. Got lots on with some other stuff because people are wondering about a lockdown because of this Covid thing."

"Well, can you expedite?" She pressed the red telephone icon to finish the call.

Jeremy glared at his mobile. "You'll just have to wait, you snotty bitch," he muttered.

***

"What the bloody hell is going on, Fred?" Douglas Yardley-Henderson stretched back in his deluxe leather office chair.

"The conveyancing is taking longer than we thought, the reason being is that there could well be a lockdown and everyone wants their conveyancing work completed as quickly as possible."

"Jesus wept!" Douglas sighed. "You also said in your message that the access roads came up for discussion at the Stonechester Borough Council meeting. So?"

"Well, there was a lot of discussion and a few council members are against it. They've been reading the social media accounts of the PVP lot, so know that there's going to be warehousing and a solar panel farm even though there's nothing official. A couple of them are married to the PVP members so know exactly what's going on. A reporter from the Stonechester Gazette also turned up and was taking notes. They've never really bothered before."

"Well, a meeting about public conveniences and litter bins isn't going to sell a lot of newspapers, is it?"

"Doug, this is getting really heavy now." Fred's voice began to quaver.

"Oh for fuck's sake, Fred." Douglas sat upright and slapped his desk in frustration. "You knew this would happen at some stage. So, OK, now it's official. The Tilley/Drage lands are going to be developed for warehousing and a solar panel farm and there'll be two access roads. So what? You're on the Norssex County Council as well as the leader of the Stonechester Borough Council. You know who to speak to, to get outline planning permission. Get a bloody grip, you stupid, silly bastard."

"Don't speak to me like that. I've worked bloody hard to get us this far. You need me, Doug. You need me. Don't bloody forget it." Fred's voice had taken on an unusually determined tone.

"Yeah, I need you like I need a hole in the head." Douglas lay back in his leather chair again. "Before you kick off again, Fred. I've got some good news which makes a welcome change from your messages of bloody doom and gloom."

Fred was shaking with rage. It took all his willpower to reply. "What's that, then?"

Douglas laughed. "You know that Saudi owned supermarket chain, Al-defidel Well, they're interested in building a brand-new branch beside the access road to the A6. I approached them and told them about the warehouses, so it's a no brainer to offer cheap shopping on site to the warehouse operatives."

"Oh."

"Is that all you can say, Fred? Christ almighty, here I am, working my arse off and that's all you can say, oh. So, pull your fucking finger out, Fred. This'll mean more dosh for us both." Fred exhaled.

"OK, Doug. Leave it with me. I'm on it."

"Yeah, yeah and the rest. Bye."

Fred switched off his mobile. He took a deep breath in and out in an effort to compose himself and then wandered into the living room. Edna was sitting in her favourite armchair, knitting.

"OK, dear?"

"Yes. It's just work. You know, the usual. Council stuff."

Edna didn't look up from her knitting. "Yes, I know. Just council stuff."

***

St Agatha's was packed and buzzing. A fourth tea urn had been purchased and was now alongside the other three, steam gently rattling the lids. Barbera had managed to find a third volunteer to (wo)man the serving of hot drinks and biscuits.

Lady Caroline was still hors de combat in that she couldn't manage the pulpit stairs, for which Reverend Fuller gave quiet thanks. She also found sitting in the pew on Sunday most uncomfortable so had elected to stay at home this evening; Sir Henry had promised to give her comprehensive feedback. Meanwhile, he was chatting to that very attractive lady from the yoga club.

So it was that Mandy Culverhouse found herself taking charge of the PVP meeting for a second time. Resuming her spot at the top of the middle aisle, she called out for everyone's attention which she was given almost immediately.

"Thank you all for coming here tonight. I think this may be the last time we can meet all together. As you know, there's likely to be a lockdown shortly. For how long? Well, nobody knows at the moment, but let's keep our fingers crossed that it won't be too long."

She gazed around at the many faces: middle-aged, old, rather old, very old, a few people in their twenties and thirties. It didn't matter. They cared and cared enough to leave the latest woes of 'Eastenders' and 'Coronation Street' behind them and turn out on a cold spring evening. Thank God St Agatha's had decent heating.

"The latest news is that the land registry now shows Ted Drage's land to be owned by DAYH Investments. My husband told me this evening." There was dead silence. Nobody stirred.

"The second item to tell you is that the Stonechester Borough Council minutes show that not just one, but two access roads will be built to serve warehousing and a solar panel farm. My husband tells me that because of the acreage involved and the fact that most of it is agricultural land, it has to go out to public consultation, and also, it has to be discussed at county level, so Norssex County Council will become involved, especially as outline planning permission is required. If they're not already, that is."

There were a few moments of silence and then everyone began talking. Rita stood up beside her friend and yelled out, "Shut up, everyone. Just shut up for a couple of minutes, and then you can all have your say!"

Gradually, the babble died down. Mandy went to continue but Rita cut across her.

"Right, everybody, you've heard the latest. Now it's gone public, we can all do something about it. The plans have to be published and put in public places, so we can have a look. We can object and I can tell you all that I shall be objecting in the strongest possible terms."

Mandy was staring at her friend in amazement. Where had all this come from?

A hand shot up and its owner stood up. It was one of Brian's fellow twitchers.

"Hi, all. Me name's Jim Hunter. How do you propose to object then?"

Mandy quickly glanced at Rita, in case she wanted to continue, but Rita was staring at Jim.

"Well, there'll be a petition, on-line, that everyone can sign. I'm sure the *Stonechester Gazette* will be covering the story as it evolves." Terry Bailey stood up and waved.

"You bet, Mandy. It's going to get full coverage. And we'll get the *Norbrough Chronicle* lot involved too."

"I'll organise the on-line petition," called out Kevin Miller from one of the side pews.

"Thank you all for that," said Mandy. "The thing is, if there is a lockdown, we will all have to keep in touch by computer or mobile. So, what I suggest is that we all check the PVP social media accounts every day and add in anything of interest. For instance, Brian, if you see anybody measuring up or any strangers when you and the guys are birdwatching."

"No probs, Mandy," called Brian and there was a rumble of agreement from his fellow twitchers.

"The other thing we can use, apart from our usual *WhatsApp* group, is *Zoom*. Using *Zoom,* we can see each other and show things as they happen which you can't with *WhatsApp.*"

"What's *Zoom?*" somebody called out. Kevin Miller stood up and addressed the church.

"I work in IT, you know, with computers and I'd be very happy to download the app and show you how to work it. Come and see me when we break for drinks."

"Thanks so much, Kevin. That's really kind of you," said Mandy. Letty Miller, sitting in a side pew with Betty and Hetty, nudged them both and said, "that's my wonderful boy, that is."

"OK, everyone. Before we break for drinks, does anybody have anything to say or any questions?"

A hand shot up and a man stood up. "Yes, I do. Do you think that a lockdown will slow everything down? You know, all this planning permission stuff?"

"I don't know, to be honest. I don't think anybody does, really. If the country is locked down, then I suppose nothing much will happen until it's, well, unlocked."

Again there was silence. Barbera Fuller decided to take the bull by the horns.

"Ladies and gentlemen," she called out. "The water in the urns is boiling nicely. Please come and get your tea, coffee and biscuits."

In the general hubbub and mass exodus towards the urns and ginger nuts, Mandy looked at Rita.

"I don't know what we've started but we've started something," she said. Rita nodded smiling at Lorraine and Brian as they walked past and then turned to her friend. "And about bloody time, Mandy."

***

Felicity Holmes kept staring at her bank statement, the figure of £672,000 seemed to be typed in neon lights. Jeremy Fisher had phoned her to say the agreed selling price had been transferred to her bank account and here it was. Suddenly shaky with all the adrenaline pumping through her, she sat down. Wow! She was rich. Very rich. Made up for life. Now she could say goodbye to Stoke Newington and Edmonton and go and live anywhere she wanted to. Felicity Holmes had already made plans. Now she could put them into action.

March, 2020

Lockdown. Although almost everyone knew it was inevitable, it still caused shockwaves throughout the country.

In Norbrough, Sara Rollins had long prepared for this eventuality. Immediately, the government website offering financial support for businesses opened, she applied and managed to put in a claim before it crashed.

Her four members of staff were unsurprised but sad when she closed the club. Sara was a good employer, firm and fair. The Dick vins Dyke Club was a fun place whether you were a customer or staff. So when she told them that they would still receive their salaries, they trusted her implicitly.

Sara was more concerned about Jo who had been under a lot of pressure preparing for the Ofsted inspection that had taken place at the end of February. Now her school was closed, Jo and her fellow teachers were trying to organise home tuition for every child. And, of course, the longed for holiday at Easter was now out of the question.

As she sat watching the Six O'clock News, waiting for Jo to finish a phone call to one of her staff, Sara decided that she was going to use lockdown time to do something positive.

***

"Doug, there's nothing more I can do!" Fred Denton was trying to explain to a very unhappy Douglas Yardley-Henderson that because of lockdown, all council business was on hold until clarification had been received from central government.

"Fred, I've got my investors and the developers on my back. Now we've got the land, they want to get going. They won't pay us until we get the outline planning permission. So I'm out of pocket big-time."

"Don't you think I know that, Doug?" Fred spluttered into his mobile. "But we're all stuck at home for Christ knows how long. I can't do anything until I hear from the county council as to how we're going to be working during lockdown."

Douglas spat an expletive down the phone and hung up.

Edna Denton had been listening to Fred's conversation with Douglas. She had always made it a habit to eavesdrop his calls. It kept her in the loop, as she called it, as Fred had never ever talked about his job. In fact, Fred never really talked to her at all. She tiptoed back to her favourite armchair and resumed knitting as Fred entered their lounge. He sat down looking glum.

"Council business, dear?"

"Yes. Council business." He picked up the *Daily Express* and began reading it. Edna looked up from her knitting at the man sitting across from her. The look she gave him was venomous. She resembled Madame Defarge eyeing up the queue for the guillotine. She knew much more about 'council business' than he could ever begin to guess.

***

Eve Yardley-Henderson was unused to having her husband around full-time and she was irritated. Irritated by his tantrums, his curt manner during the numerous phone calls he made and, worse, his gauche attempts at physical romance.

Eve knew he had a mistress or even mistresses, and she was happy to let her or them cater to Doug's physical demands. In a way she was sorry for them because he really was a lousy lover. She could only assume that money from his side overcame any 'dissatisfaction' on theirs.

Up until lockdown, she had been a free agent. There had been dinner parties to organise, lunches with the wives of the well-heeled, weekly beauty treatments, hair appointments, badminton and tennis matches at the Norbrough Cricket Club, liaison with the local Conservative Party HQ now that Doug was a candidate for the Stonechester seat, and just living a life of leisure, coming and going as she pleased that also included some enjoyable off court sessions with that hunky tennis coach.

Eve knew Douglas was a lying, two-faced and ambitious bastard, as she thought him, and utterly up his own arse but that made him ideal MP material and, hopefully, a future cabinet minister, if not Prime Minister.

So, she sighed again as he flung himself around the lodge like a toddler who had lost his favourite teddy, and continued to despise him from a distance, in this case from the drawing room, aided by the latest offering from E L James.

***

"God, I miss you, darling," crooned Douglas into his mobile. Eve had gone out for a walk on her own, and he had taken advantage of her absence to ring Sonia.

"Doug, I miss you too," she crooned back. If he believed that, he'd believe anything since his ego was loads bigger than his IQ…

"Did you manage to speak to your solicitor before lockdown, as you said, you would?"

"Yes, I did actually, babe. If we jointly apply for a divorce, then we have to discuss splitting our joint assets. She is legally entitled to half of everything. That would usually take about six months. If I just apply and she contests it, then it'll take much longer."

"Well everybody knows that, Doug. That's why you should go for a quickie divorce. Offer to pay her off. Give her the lodge. Do bloody something."

"The problem is my candidacy for the Stonechester MP vacancy. My success depends on being a happily married man with a supportive wife. Eve has done a lot of networking. She has lots of contacts in both the Commons and the Lords. That's why my name was put forward."

"Christ, Doug! How much longer do I have to wait?" Sonia exploded.

For once, Douglas spoke calmly and slowly, "You'll have to wait as long as it takes, babe. We've now got a lockdown and everything has ground to a halt. Divorce proceedings, Outline Planning Permission and everything else. It's wait and see time."

Mollified by his unusually mellow tone, Sonia sighed. "OK, Doug. OK. Let's wait and see."

***

The Stonechester and District Wellbeing Walkers were taking advantage of some lovely spring weather to walk along the Pyddel Valley and up onto the wold. They were keeping more than the prerequisite two metres apart and since there were about twenty of them, they resembled a conga line snaking its way along the footpath. Quite a few of them were wearing face masks and this made conversation difficult, as did the last steep climb onto the wold summit.

Mandy was pleased in a way. The silence allowed her time to think. Mike was working from home nowadays, but he was still able to keep her briefed of any developments. Rita walked silently beside her wearing a 'Say No to Covid' face mask. She and Len were worried about the loss of business. The Cat and Cradle was empty and silent. It was so strange that she felt uncomfortable.

Len had applied to the government on-line for financial support but the lack of income, and having to still pay their staff, was keeping him awake at night.

Rita, being Rita, had taken the opportunity to give the Cat and Cradle a good clean and a touch of some much needed paint. Fabian, the chef, had spent a whole day going to town in the kitchen and everything gleamed from floor to ceiling. Rita tipped him £100 in cash by way of thanks; she felt it was only fair but she didn't tell Len. Len did not do extras.

The rest of the staff said they were looking forward to returning as soon as they were allowed to do so which Rita thought was really nice of them but, all in all, the whole situation was worrying.

"It's lovely here today, Mandy. Look at the view."

They stopped, as did the other walkers assiduously maintaining the two plus metres distance, and Rita waved her hand towards the horizon. "Wonderful," Mandy agreed. There was a Mexican Wave of nodding heads as her adjective was passed along the line. Everyone stood and looked out over the Pyddel Valley. Somebody at the back must have said, "Yes, it's lovely," as this was passed back along the line to the front in the same way.

Mandy set off again, the conga line following obediently behind her. When they arrived back at Lower Pyddelham, Mandy asked for everyone's attention.

"First of all, many thanks for joining the walk today. I do hope you have enjoyed it."

There was nodding and the odd 'I certainly did' muffled somewhat by face masks and the two metres plus distancing.

"Secondly, unfortunately we can't go anywhere for a cuppa so if you've brought a flask with you, now's the time to enjoy it. And…" She quickly added before everybody galloped off towards their cars and the promise of a hot drink. "Just a reminder that all the latest information on the PVP can be found in our new website www.pyddelvalleyprotest.co.uk. We still use our *Facebook* page too, but Kevin Miller, Letty's son, thought it'd be more professional to have a website so that our protest can go further afield than stay just locally. The details are on our *Facebook* page."

She looked around at their faces, many of them looking as if they were off to rob a bank. She smiled to herself.

"Have a good week, everyone, and see you here outside St Agatha's next Tuesday. God bless and stay safe." There were some muffled and distant goodbyes in reply and everybody headed for their cars. Rita stayed. She regarded her friend solemnly over her mask.

"Mandy, what do you think's going to happen?" Mandy shrugged.

"What do you mean? The development? Well, everything's on hold because of lockdown, so that's something, I suppose. As regards Covid, I honestly haven't a clue, love. It's highly contagious and it's killing so many people. The poor NHS can't cope. Mike told me that both Norbrough and Stonechester general hospitals are overwhelmed. Kevin Miller put it on *Facebook* that he's hardly seen his partner, Steve; the guy's working all hours."

"Yes, and Reverend Fuller wrote his sister has it. She's at home, isolating. A few others have caught it and Julia, you know her from the stables, is in hospital with it."

"Yes, I read it on our *Facebook* page. To be honest, I think quite a few people we know will be affected. Let's hope and pray that if they do, they recover." Rita nodded.

"It's terrible to see the news, lately. So many people dying and their poor families can't visit. They can't even go to the funerals."

"I feel for the NHS staff who are nursing them. They really are wonderful. Rita, we must just keep ourselves safe and hope for the best. I'm off home now and then to Tescos."

"Don't forget your mask, Mandy."

"No, I won't. I keep a packet in the car and a bottle of antiseptic handwash. Take care, Rita."

"You, too, love."

April, 2020

Felicity Holmes was furious. Furious at Fate. Furious that she was unable to go on a wonderful holiday, to fly to the Caribbean in first class and cruise around the islands. Furious that she was still stuck in her shitty little Edmonton flat but also relieved she hadn't given her landlord notice, otherwise God knows where she would have to spend lockdown.

The doorbell rang. She leaned out of her bathroom window to see who it was. There was a man and a woman, both wearing face masks, standing by the front door. Hearing the window open, they both looked up.

"Miss Felicity Holmes?"

"Yes. Who are you?"

"We're from the Serious Fraud Office and National Crime Agency. We do have ID. We would just like to ask you a few questions," answered the woman. Felicity went cold inside.

"Er, OK. Let me put a mask on and I'll come down." She was shaking as she slipped the loops around her ears. She descended the stairs in a daze and opened the door. The woman's black eyes regarded her interestedly above her mask and the man nodded. They showed her their IDs.

"I suppose you'd best come upstairs. To my flat." They followed her back up the stairs and into her living room. They both sat on the two-seater settee whilst Felicity sat in her armchair.

"Apologies for disturbing you but we work even in a lockdown," the woman explained.

"What, what do you want?" She eyed them over her mask nervously.

"You are Miss Felicity Anne Holmes?" asked the man. She nodded. The woman sat and observed her with those unblinking black eyes. He continued, "Your uncle, Edward Anthony Drage, died last year and you were the only beneficiary to his estate. Is that correct?" Felicity nodded.

"Yes, according to the solicitors, I was. I mean, I am."

"Can you confirm the name of the solicitors, please."

"Yes. It was Harding, Russell in Stonechester. Apparently, they were my uncle's solicitors and I received a letter from them telling me that he had died and left everything in his will to me. Do you want to see the letter?" the woman replied.

"Yes, please, Miss Holmes." Felicity went into the tiny kitchen and pulled a large envelope from behind the kettle. It contained all the paperwork from Harding, Russell. She handed it to the woman. "Everything's in that," she said.

"Thank you, Miss Holmes." The woman handed the envelope to her companion.

"We will be keeping the originals but will post you photocopies," she explained. "The reason for this is that we believe your uncle was involved in not only defrauding Defra but also in handling stolen farm machinery. In consequence, he was able to leave you a substantial sum of money. Did you or do you know anything about this?"

"God, no! Oh, Christ! This is awful! No, I didn't have any idea the money came from crime! Oh Jesus!" Felicity had begun to shake visibly. The woman nodded.

"Thank you, Miss Holmes. Greg, perhaps you could get this lady a glass of water." The man stood up and went into the kitchen, returning with a mug of water. Felicity took it gratefully and managed not to spill its contents as she lifted her mask and drank. The woman began the questioning.

"Had you any contact with your uncle during the past, say, decade or so?" Felicity shook her head.

"No, none at all. The last time I saw him was when my Aunty Viv died. She was my mum's sister, and I used to go and stay with them on the farm during the school holidays. I was fourteen when she died and after her funeral, Mum and I never had any contact with him. Mum never liked him. Come to that, I didn't much either. But I loved Aunty Viv. She was wonderful."

"So, Harding, Russell, as your uncle's executors, wrote to you. I believe they also organised your uncle's funeral."

"Yes, that's right. Not that there was much to organise. There were only three of us there, apart from the funeral director's people." Felicity took a gulp of water.

"Tell me about the two other people."

"Well, what I can remember is that one was young and very well-spoken and the other man was much older and fatter. The young one gave me his card. It's in that envelope. He said they were interested in buying my uncle's land if I was interested in selling. That's about it really."

"Have either of them, or both, approached you since that day?"

"No. All my dealings have been with Harding, Russell. A Christiana Morleigh did the probate and a guy called Fisher did the conveyancing. I agreed that Harding, Russell could act as intermediaries in the sale because she said, that is Christiana, said that if I wanted to sell, she knew of some people who were keen to buy it. I didn't want to farm the land, so I said yes, go ahead."

"And all the documentation from both the probate and land sale are here in this envelope?"

Felicity nodded.

"Thank you, Miss Holmes. I don't think we need any more information, for the moment. However," the woman gave Felicity a hard look over her mask. "When lockdown is over, please don't try and leave the country." She stood up, as did the man. He added, "Thank you for your time. Much appreciated." Felicity went to get up too but the woman held up her hand. "No, we'll see ourselves out."

They left. She heard the front door close and through the bathroom window saw them walk up the street and get into a car. Then she put her head above the toilet and threw up.

***

"Did you record all that, Greg?" He nodded as he drove them towards the North Circular.

"Excellent. We've got incontrovertible evidence now." She smiled behind her mask and sat in silence as he drove them back to Cockspur Street.

June, 2020

Len Sharman was a happy and relieved man. Rishi Sunak's 'Eat to Help Out' campaign had come as a godsend. The Cat and Cradle was alive again even though only six people were allowed in at any one time. However, Len had got around that by putting picnic benches three metres apart in the carpark so that patrons could eat and enjoy their meal *al fresco* in separation and comparative safety.

Rita was pleased too, even though she wasn't able to remove her face mask for most of the day. It was also great to sit and chat with Mandy in the sunshine and hear the latest news – which wasn't at all good. So many mutual acquaintances they knew had died. Julia Carrington-Herbert from the stables was one and Tom Healey another. Kevin Miller was distraught: Steve had caught Covid and was in Norbrough ICU. Barbera Fuller had been admitted to Stonechester General but was now home recovering slowly. Reverend Fuller was still concerned about her well-being but was busy with several funerals, with dispensing love and comfort to all, and visiting those of his parishioners who were unable to leave their homes, as well as other pastoral duties.

Despite all the terrible news, there were some gleams of compassionate sunshine. The PVP *Facebook* page and the website had proved to be a very popular and effective means of local communication. Letty Miller reported on *Facebook* that Kevin was helping the owner of the Dick vins Dyke Club in Norbrough, who had been cooking and delivering free meals for OAPs and other vulnerable people in the area. Susan Sudborough had written that 'Good Days' coffee shop in Stonechester had gone mobile and had been serving free hot drinks to NHS staff outside Stonechester General Hospital and also to a couple of care homes. Hetty Hodson wrote that in Stonechester, a food bank had been set up and volunteers there included Muslims, Hindus and Sikhs, as well as members of the Sally Army and local churches.

There were other stories of small kindnesses that were heartening to read, like somebody offering to take people's dogs for a walk or run errands or just chat through an open window.

Brian Ramsbottom was posting weekly reports on the bird life which had apparently increased during lockdown, and Kevin had posted a video showing the beauty of the Pyddel Valley and the wold on the PVP *Facebook* page which had initiated a torrent of 'likes'.

As far as the *Stonechester Gazette* was concerned, Terry Bailey had written several articles about the PVP but was forced to choose his words carefully in case of potential libel. He told Mandy and Rita that he couldn't do much more until the council meetings resumed, but at least the PVP now had county coverage as the *Norbrough Chronicle* had also picked up the story.

The online petition set up by Kevin Miller had attracted over a thousand signatures and there had been thousands of hits on the PVP website and *Facebook* page. All in all, their campaign was proving successful.

October, 2020

Felicity Holmes was feeling rather unwell. In fact, she'd been off colour since the visit by the SFO and NCA people but today she had a temperature, a cough and couldn't taste anything.

She realised that, somehow, she'd caught Covid. She supposed that it was that night out with three of her friends. They'd all been determined to have a good time after being cooped up for so long. Felicity, in particular, wanted to try and forget 'that visit' for a couple of hours; it had been haunting her ever since. That woman's eyes. Horrible!

The pub had been busy; the food had been quite good and the drinks had just flowed. She couldn't quite remember how she got home but she knew she'd had a great time. Now she was paying for it.

She phoned up her friend Sharon to see if she and the other two were OK. Sharon said she was fine, as was Hannah, but Maddie wasn't feeling too good either. Felicity told her she was going to isolate and took to her bed. She began to find breathing difficult but persevered with Vicks and lots of hot drinks and paracetamol. During the night, her breathing deteriorated. She tried to get out of bed to get her mobile to ring for an ambulance but tripped over the bedside rug and fell, hitting her head on the chest of drawers.

A few days later, Sharon phoned to see how she was and to say that Maddie was in hospital. Her call went to leave a message. She tried again and texted but there was no response. Worried, Sharon went to Felicity's flat but nobody answered the door. Thoroughly alarmed now, Sharon called the police who broke in. They found Felicity on the floor in her bedroom. Dead!

***

"Felicity Holmes is dead," said Greg into his mobile. He was standing outside her flat watching as a body bag was placed inside the ambulance by a crew in full PPE.

"How?"

"Covid and a fall. She apparently cracked her head on a chest of drawers. The cops think she tripped up on a rug cos it was all rumpled under her feet."

"Poor girl. Shame. Right, Greg, get a copy of the death certificate as soon as possible and then I'll apply to the Director to sequester her bank account. You can stand down now from all that hanging around Edmonton. Come back to the office and let me have a full report."

The ambulance drove off. "Will do," he responded.

"And, by the way, Greg, thank you for all your hard work on this case. Now we can really go after Y-H et al." He nearly dropped his mobile from shock. As far as he knew, she had never thanked anybody before.

November, 2020

"Another bloody lockdown," sighed Susan Sudborough to her husband, Stan. "It's been ages since we had a meeting of the Historical Society. Doing it by *Zoom* isn't the same, really."

"Never mind, love. They reckon they've found a vaccine for Covid, so perhaps, things are looking up a bit."

"I suppose so. Stan love, June, Clare and me are going for a walk on the wold tomorrow morning. Clare's husband treated her to a metal detector for her birthday and we're going to try it out."

"Well happy hunting, love. You never know, you might dig up some treasure!" He grinned at her and returned to watching the ten o'clock news.

***

Clare Capps began walking in straight lines across the top of the wold, the metal detector held in front of her, her forehead furrowed in concentration, alert for any bleeps. Susan and June Packwood stood watching her, well wrapped up against the chilly breeze. They had already bumped into Brian Ramsbottom and four of his fellow twitchers in the valley below. Susan was holding a spade ready to dig up anything the detector might reveal.

Suddenly, they heard bleeping and rushed over to Clare who had begun to scrabble in the mud. It was a horseshoe.

"Well, at least we know it works," said June. They continued and, after an hour or so, had managed to add some nails, an old penny and a couple of beer can tabs to the collection. They decided to stop and have a hot drink. June poured some very welcome coffee from the large flask into the three mugs she had brought with her.

"Clare, try over there, by those bumps and ridges," Susan suggested. "I've always thought there might be something worth digging up."

"OK but I'm feeling really cold now. If we don't find anything in the next half an hour, I'm going to call it a day."

They wandered over to the spot, Susan had indicated, and Clare began to amble up and down in straight lines once again, trying not to trip up on the uneven ground. Susan, just to keep warm, began digging at a particularly prominent bump. Yes, there was definitely some sort of wall here. She continued and found that the wall made a right-angled turn. Suddenly, she felt a rush of heat and excitement that wasn't a hot flush; it quite drove away the cold.

"June, I think we've got something. Look!" June looked.

"It might be an old farm building or something."

"What up here? The ground falls away quite steeply over there." June was looking doubtful when the detector began bleeping. Clare was beckoning them urgently.

"Look, girls!" She was grinning from ear to ear. "We've got a find!" She held out her hand. Two arrowheads.

"Oh, wow!" This from June. "Keep going, Clare. See if we find anything else." Clare began waving the detector over another furrow nearby and Susan began digging the spot where Clare had found the arrowheads. Almost simultaneously, Susan squealed and the detector bleeped, making June jump.

"Coins, coins! Oh, my God, just look!" There in the earth lay about ten coins. Susan picked one up and spat on it wiping away the mud with a tissue. She and June could just make out a mediaeval king's head. They both stared at it in shock.

"Are you two going to come over here?" Clare called to them crossly.

"Oh right. Sorry, love." The ground was very uneven, so they picked their way carefully. Clare pointed to a dip in the earth.

"Dig that, Susan." Susan began to carefully clear away the surface. The November day was beginning to bleed into a grey dusk, but excitement drove them on.

"It's a bit of sword pommel, I'm sure," said Susan.

"Do you know how old?" asked June.

"No idea. Look, girls. We've obviously found a site of some kind. We must report this to the Norssex

Council's Finds Liaison Officer and the Coroner, too, within fourteen days. I'll do that when I get home."

"Are you going to look after our finds?" asked Clare.

"Yes, I'll do that. I've got some tissue paper here, and then I'll pop them in my Tupperware box."

"We can't do much more. The light's going," Clare said. "Let's call it a day."

Once the finds were safely packed away, the three ladies made their way down the path and back to their cars.

"Do you want to put this out to the PVP *Facebook* page?" asked June, getting into her Micra.

"No, don't say anything for the moment," Susan replied. "Let me report it first to the authorities and see what they say. I'll ring you both tomorrow, and let you know. Well done, girls! Especially you, Clare. We couldn't have done it without you and your detector." Clare grinned.

"Well, it's about time Tony bought me something useful for a birthday present. Usually, it's perfume or flowers or both."

"You're bloody lucky, love," June said. "Bob usually forgets my birthday, so I get sod all."

They drove off to their respective homes in Stonechester, excited at the prospect of what the following days would bring. A second lockdown didn't seem so bad after all.

***

"Doug, I've got some bad news." Douglas Yardley-Henderson sighed.

"Go on, Fred."

"Some ladies from the Stonechester Historical Society discovered some ruins and archaeological finds up on the wold. It's been reported to the county coroner and also to Norssex County Council who contacted Historical England because the finds could be Saxon, apparently. They've been up there and are going to carry out a formal dig once the lockdown is over. That puts the kybosh on our application for planning permission." He waited until the blast of expletives had died down.

"There is some good news though," he said, tentatively.

"Oh, yeah, Fred. What's that then?" Doug's contempt dripped down the telephone line. Fred felt his dislike turn to raw hatred.

"The site is right on the edge of the wold, overlooking the valley, so it doesn't impact too badly on our plans for warehousing, although it might reduce the space for the solar panels." His tone was abrupt. It was so unlike Fred that Douglas, at the other end of the line, did a double-take. In a more placatory tone, he asked, "So, what's been happening at the council meetings? You've been Zooming, haven't you?"

"Yes, but both the Norssex and Stonechester meetings have kept business to a minimum. We've only been dealing with very urgent stuff. I'm afraid our application wasn't considered urgent." This released another torrent of expletives. Fred glared at his receiver and put the phone down. Doug, you really are a total piece of shit, he thought.

Turning around, he saw Edna standing by the lounge door. She smiled at him and handed him a glass of Chivas Regal, his favourite tipple.

"Thank you, dear." He shrugged his shoulders and took a large mouthful.

"Council business?" she asked. "Yes, dear, just council business."

***

All the members of the Stonechester Historical Society were in archaeological heaven. Once confirmation had been received that Historical England would excavate the site, Susan Sudborough had posted the story of their finds on the PVP website and Facebook page. Terry Bailey had written a long article in the Stonechester Gazette, including his interview with Susan, Clare and June, and photos of their finds which had been confirmed as being from the early twelfth century. This had initiated lots of 'likes' on Facebook and hits on the PVP website.

The Wellbeing Walkers' conga line had wound straight to the site, and they were all staring at the ridges and dips in the ground. After a while, somebody said, "I can see what Susan means. All those funny shapes. I mean, it's not flat, is it?"

After another while, someone else said, "I wonder what them lumps are."

Then, a few moments later, another asked plaintively, "Can we go back now. It's so cold up here." At which point, the conga line about turned and retraced its steps back down the path to Lower Pyddleham and the warmth of their cars.

December, 2020

This month brought the wonderful news that there were a couple of vaccines and the government hoped to make them available to the public in January. Meanwhile, most people were preparing to make the best of what would be a very restricted Christmas.

Len Sharman was glum again. The Cat and Cradle was beginning to lose money despite his parsimony. He was even getting on Rita's nerves.

"Honestly," she told Mandy from her mobile. "He's such a miserable git nowadays. I shouldn't say this about my husband but it's like living with a wet weekend."

"Never mind, love. Once we get our inoculations, everyone's businesses will pick up. Surely, he's getting financial help from the government?"

"Yes, we are but he hates it that the place is virtually empty, most of the time."

Other people were becoming bored, too. Barbera Fuller had recovered from Covid but she still experienced shortness of breath and fatigue. She felt frustrated because there was so much to do now that it was Christmas. Michael was working so hard and she could only give limited help.

Eve Yardley-Henderson was bored to the back teeth. Doug was driving her mad, moping about the Lodge, occasionally making and taking phone calls. She was unable to escape. There were no massages, no hairdressers, no manicures and pedicures, no sex with the tennis coach. Worst, there were no social events. Usually, at this time of year, she was a major hostess, entertaining the great and the good of the county, as well as MPs and very senior civil servants. Really, life had become extremely tedious.

Sara Rollins had experienced many emotions in the past year but none of them was boredom. She and her staff had been extremely busy throughout the lockdowns, preparing free meals for the vulnerable. Not normally upset by the suffering of others, she had been moved by the plight of the people she had been helping. She had also been moved by the people manning the Norbrough food bank and had taken them hot snacks and drinks. As she remarked to Jo, "It's about bloody time I put something back."

Steve Barlow had died from Covid. Kevin was inconsolable. He joined his parents' bubble so that he didn't spend Christmas alone. There wasn't anything Letty or her husband could say or do but they were wise enough just to be there for him.

All in all, the festive season came and went quietly for most people. They were all wondering what lay in wait for them in 2021.

January, 2021

"I've had the jab, me duck," Winnie Jenkinson called out triumphantly to Reverend Fuller as she slowly lowered herself down into her usual pew. "Me arm aches now but I don't care."

"Well done, Winnie. I'm very pleased for you. It's a sort of an eighty-first birthday present."

"I don't think much of it being a present but I'm so grateful to get it. How's your Barbera?"

"I'm getting there, Winnie." Barbera had slowly made her way across the church; she now used a walking stick. It helped with her mobility.

"We're in the right place to say thank you, we are, me duck," said Winnie. Reverend Fuller nodded.

"We certainly are." The other four people at Evensong had spaced themselves out in the pews. Six people is better than no people, he thought, remembering how full it had been just over a year ago. So many of them had succumbed to Covid. He prayed the new vaccines would be a success.

***

In Cockspur Street, the Serious Fraud Office had never slept, Christmas, lockdown or no lockdown.

Investigations and evidence-gathering continued. Greg had taken some leave during the festive season and returned to the office to find her poring over various papers. He wondered if she had ever left.

"Happy New Year," he offered brightly through his facemask. She didn't look up. He sat down in a chair opposite.

"Well, this new lockdown will slow things up even more with the Yardley-Henderson case. By the way, some local ladies have discovered an archaeological site that Historical England are going to excavate. That will slow things up even more. Yardley-Henderson et al must be going nuts. This gives us more time." For the first time, she looked up at him over her mask. "Hopefully, we'll get authority to sequester the Holmes bank account."

Greg nodded. She continued, "The Norssex and Stonechester council meetings have been briefed via *Zoom,* and there's been no discussion regarding the warehousing development application. Again, once this lockdown has been lifted, I expect Fred Denton to start pushing that through. Anything on Russell, Harding?" Greg shook his head.

"No. They've all been working from home, and my contact there tells me it's been nothing special. Just wills and probate. They've been busy there, as you can imagine." He'd phoned up Yvonne, the receptionist, who'd been thrilled to hear from him. It didn't take much for her to spill the latest Russell, Harding beans.

"Right. That's about it for now." She stood up and went and put on her coat. "I'm off to get my Covid jab. Have you had yours yet?"

"No, not yet."

"Well, I suggest you do so. Just show any clinic your warrant card and they'll do it there and then."

"Will do."

***

Christiana Morleigh swore. She hated working from home, she hated probate, she hated lockdown, she hated not being paid her share of the deal.

She had been regularly checking the PVP website and *Facebook* page, as well as the on-line petition, and had been horrified to see how many people had signed it. She had always considered the population of Norssex to be sub-normal and was shocked at how well organised the PVP was.

She had phoned Fred Denton a couple of times since Christmas to see if there had been any progress in the application for planning permission. His answers frustrated and angered her even though she had received a sugar-coated £10,000 to keep her sweet.

She sat deep in thought by her laptop, then began typing. Perhaps, a little blackmail might expedite matters.

***

Douglas Yardley-Henderson stared at the rain falling on the drawing room window. He wanted to scream. He hated not being in control. Fuck lockdowns.

Eve was being particularly difficult. She was obviously finding living in such close proximity with him onerous. He only saw her at mealtimes and, sometimes, not even then. She had moved into the spare suite, making it quite clear it was off limits to him, so he couldn't even get his leg over to pass the time and ease his general frustration.

Christmas and New Year had hardly been the season of good cheer then. He could only hope that the new vaccines would bring lockdown to a complete and speedy end. To cheer himself up, he thought of the millions he was going to make from the deal and planned how he was going to spend it. His plans did not include Eve.

February, 2021

The NHS Covid vaccination campaign was going well in Norssex. All the clinics were very busy so there was always a bit of a wait. Mandy and Mike Culverhouse sat together in the queue waiting for their turn.

"Who would've thought this would happen? You know, the whole Covid thing," said Mandy. Mike shrugged.

"I don't know, love. I'm just so grateful that we're both here to get the jab."

"Will you look forward to going back to work once lockdown is over?" He smiled at her through his facemask; she could tell he was smiling by his eyes.

"You know what, Mandy. I love being at home with you. I can't wait until I retire, to be honest."

"What a lovely thing to say, Mike!" She felt herself begin to well up. He nudged her affectionately.

"It's not long to go, love. Only another two years."

"Yes, I know but a lot can happen in two years. Just look at what's happened in the last two."

"Yes, but let's be positive. Let's…"

"Mr Michael James Culverhouse, please." One of the nurses had called out his name. Mike stood up. "I'm here." He began rolling up his sleeve as he made his way over to her desk.

"Mrs Amanda Anne Culverhouse, please. Good afternoon. Come this way." Mandy stood up and followed a nurse over to another desk. How fortunate they were to have survived and to be given this chance of a vaccination. God bless the NHS!

March, 2021

"Have you told her yet, Doug?"

They were both lying in bed in a small hotel in, of all places, Brighton. *Typical bloody Doug,* she thought. Talk about a cliché. She suddenly felt cheap and used. Pushing the feeling aside, she turned on her side to face him.

"No, not yet. I will though, I promise." He continued to stare up at the ceiling. It took all her self-control not to slap him.

"You've been saying that for nearly a year." At last, he turned his head and looked at her.

"This lockdown has slowed everything up. Everything. The land deal, the divorce. Everything." She was surprised to see him looking rather frightened.

"Doug, I've had enough. The solicitor has told you what you have to do. You tell her when you get home tomorrow, and I'll meet you on Friday. No doubt she'll kick you out so you can move in with me."

He sighed. The Stonechester Conservative Club Committee was due to elect their new MP, the following week. It was important that he and Eve appeared to be the perfect married couple. He knew she would go ballistic if he told her about Sonia after all the work and effort she had put in during the past four years or so. Besides, if the committee found out that he had a mistress and his marriage was over, so would his bid to become an MP. Sonia's voice cut across his thoughts.

"Doug, listen to me, and listen to me good. If you don't leave Eve, I will go to the police and tell them about your dodgy money-making schemes and…"

"You're blackmailing me?" He looked at her in horror. Her face left him no doubt that she meant every word.

"Whatever you want to call it. I've waited too long and you've broken too many promises."

"You two-faced, conniving fuc…" Sonia got up and began dressing. She laughed. It wasn't a nice laugh. She didn't bother looking at him.

"Two-faced? Conniving? That's rich coming from you, Doug." As she pulled on her coat and picked up her bag, she laughed again.

"This Friday at 11:00 a.m. There's a nice coffee shop in Meeting Lane, Stonechester called 'Good Days'. Be there and be sure that Eve knows you're leaving her." She left the room, slamming the door behind her. He lay on the bed feeling sick. After a few moments, he began punching the contacts list on his mobile. The number rang.

"Fred, we need to meet. Tomorrow, noon. Make it somewhere quiet. Yeah, that's fine. See you, then."

***

They were in Fred Denton's back garden. Edna Denton had gone out shopping.

"Jesus, Doug, she'll blow everything to kingdom come. We have to shut her up. How much does she know?" Fred Denton looked despairingly at Douglas who had the grace to look sheepish.

"Virtually, everything. She knows about you, Harding, Russell, the developers and where they get their money from."

"Oh, dear God! You bloody idiot." He looked heavenwards as if searching for divine intervention. Then he asked, "Can we pay her off?" Again, Douglas looked sheepish.

"The company's really low on funds, Fred. Its assets couldn't cover what she'd probably ask for." He sighed and added by way of explanation, "There's no money until the developers pay up, and they won't do that until we have planning permission. That was the agreement. So, paying that Holmes woman has cleared us out."

"Oh God!" Fred sat down suddenly on the low garden wall. "What are we going to do?"

Edna Denton standing behind the tall yew hedge, a shopping bag at her feet, smiled. "Yes," she said to herself. "What are you going to do?"

***

He found her sitting at one of the tables for two. The coffee shop was crowded. *It was always bloody crowded,* he thought. There was the hum of conversations and the occasional burst of laughter. It would be better this way;

she'd be unlikely to cause a scene in front of all these people. Or so, he hoped.

He weaved his way towards her. When she saw him, her face lit up and as he stood beside her, she smiled up at him.

"What would you like to drink, Sonia?"

"A cappuccino please, Doug."

"Anything to eat?"

"No, no thanks."

He joined the queue at the counter and soon returned with two frothy cappuccinos. Sitting down opposite, he took a sip from his cup. She didn't touch hers but looked at him expectantly.

"Did you tell her?"

He took another sip of coffee to play for time; it was far too hot to swallow properly. She seemed to sense his hesitation.

"Well?"

"She knows about us, or well, she guessed apparently." He picked up his cup and put it back down. He looked at her face but couldn't quite look her in the eye.

"She found a hotel bill. You know, the place where the conference was held and we stayed over an extra night. In one of my suits. In one of the pockets. Stupid of me, really."

He toyed with his cup, lifted it, took another sip and stole a quick glance at her. She had leaned back in her seat, her body rigid. There was no smile now, just a hard stare.

"And?"

He decided to get it over with and make a quick exit, so his next words came out in a rush.

"She said if I left her, she would make sure everyone would know that I've been having an affair. She said she would ensure that my political career as the next prospective MP for Stonechester would dive bomb. She would divorce me and take me to the cleaners, financially. Unless" – he hesitated – "unless I give you up."

He thought back to the conversation with his wife the previous evening. That was in essence what Eve had said but he had been shocked at the language she had used and how acerbic and cutting she had been about him, ending with, "If you don't give her up, you bastard, I'll make your life, private and professional, a fucking nightmare!"

Now, here in the coffee shop, their silence was so profound that both of them could hear snippets of conversations from the surrounding tables and the hiss of the coffee machine. He sneaked another glance at her. Her face was white and her eyes were like ice.

"So, this is our Last Supper, is it, Doug? A cup of coffee and now fuck off into the sunset?"

"I'm so sorry, Sonia. Truly I am. We've had some great times together, haven't we. Haven't we?"

She stood up suddenly, picked up her cup and poured the contents all over his head. She then took his cup and poured the coffee all over his lap. He yelped; the drinks were still quite hot. The white foam settled on his hair and coffee dripped down his face. His new Gieves & Hawkes suit was ruined. She gave him a nasty smile and then grinned at the nearby customers who were now looking at them, attracted by the noise. She gestured towards him.

"Ladies and gentlemen, this is Douglas Yardley-Henderson, the prospective MP for Stonechester. You are now seeing him in his true colours. Wet, pale, stained and blotchy. In fact, a right drip. And that's just his policies! That's the ins and outs of him, although it's mainly outs – he prematurely ejaculates in bed!" With that she made her way past the surrounding tables and out through the door without a backwards glance. There was some giggling as he tried to stand up with all the aplomb he could muster, but his trousers were stuck to his crotch, and some of the foam had also adhered to that area. One of the men, sitting at a nearby table with his friends, called out,
"Looks like you've had an exciting morning, mate." There was some laughter from the other tables. Shrinking from the gaze and grins of the rest of the customers, he ran from the shop.

***

"Well?" asked Eve.

"I've given her up and told her straight that our affair is over. I was really tough with her," lied Douglas. Eve knew he was lying. She had seen the state of his suit but played along.

"How did she take it?"

"Not very well, I'm afraid. She stormed off."
"Right. That's all settled then. Now, I've been in contact with Sir Henry Fryers-Faversham, and he and his wife

will be holding a cocktail party for us to meet all the Conservative Club Committee members. That's tonight at 7:00 p.m. so I suggest we put everything behind us and prepare for this evening. Wear the dark grey tweed, I think. A white shirt and Conservative blue tie would be a nice touch. And for God's sake, Doug, try and look alert and poised, as if you are already MP for Stonechester."

***

"How did you get on with her today?" asked Fred Denton. He and Douglas were each clutching a glass of Pommeroy Brut Champagne and had managed to find a quiet corner by the entrance to the conservatory while the rest of the party swirled around them.

"Badly. I gave her the heave-ho and she stormed off."

"Did she threaten you again?"

"No, she… Good evening, Lady Caroline. Thank you so much for inviting Eve and myself to this lovely soiree."

"Your wife is a delight, Douglas. By the way, I'm so proud of you, my dear nephew, for probably being the next MP for Stonechester. Your parents would've been delighted. Certainly, my sister would've been. You are a credit to our family."

"That's so kind of you. Thank you."

"Now if you'll excuse me, I must mingle." Nodding to Fred, off sailed Lady Caroline like a dreadnought at full speed to accost her other guests.

"Doug, I'm bloody worried about what she might do next."

"That makes two of us." They both stood in their corner watching the crowd. Then Fred said, "What if Christiana Morleigh and I were to have a word with her. You know, explain that we can pay her a really large sum of money, life-changing cash, if she keeps stum and waits."

Douglas looked disgusted. "She's such a bitch. She deserves nothing."

"Well, I can't think of any other way, can you? I could give her fifty grand which should keep her sweet until the planning permission comes through. She'd be bloody stupid to turn that down."

Douglas shrugged and sipped his rather warm Pommeroy. Sonia was definitely not stupid.

"OK, let's do that then. I'll leave it to you to organise. Now I must go and meet our chairman." He disappeared into a clique to be joined by Eve who was shaking various hands and laughing. Fred stood for a moment and then caught the eye of a Norssex county councillor who beckoned him over. He wondered vaguely where Edna was. She was like a chameleon, blending into the background until she was almost invisible.

The 'chameleon' emerged from behind the conservatory door. She was enjoying the champagne and the party enormously.

***

Brian Ramsbottom and a couple of his fellow twitchers were crouching in a reed bed by the mere up on the wold, watching some grey herons build a nest. It was a beautiful spring morning; the water reflected the blue sky, decorated with scudding clouds. Other birds and some ducks were busy nest building nearby but they were particularly interested in the herons. After a while, Brian remarked, "Geoff, did you have curry last night?" Geoff nodded, reddening.

"Sorry."

"Thought so," said Brian. "Thank God, we're in the open air and not in a hide. Do us all a favour, pal, and tell Mary to lay off the lentils next time."

Fred Smith began to get cramp in his legs.

"Sorry, you two, but I've got to move cos I'm in bloody agony." Geoff Tunstall tutted but Brian regarded Fred sympathetically.

"I know just what that's like. Try and stretch your legs out." Fred nodded and pulled himself out of the reed bed as quietly as he could. Once on the bank, he stood up and began to do the calf stretches his GP had showed him. It really was bloody agony. After a few moments, he felt the pain lessen. He decided to take Brian's advice and began walking along the bank. It really was a lovely day. After all the bad news, he could feel his spirits lift. He and Florrie were going for their jab tomorrow, and there was talk that the government was going to lift the lockdown. Thank God!

He came to where a stream joined the mere and some movement in the water caught his eye. Taking a closer look, he saw what he thought were some very large and colourful new lizards swimming near the bank. One of them swam on its side and Fred saw its black and yellow underside. He began to feel very excited. Could they be? Could they really be?

He ran back to the others as fast as his sore calves would allow.

"Brian, Geoff!"

"Oh, for Christ's sake, shut up, Fred," hissed Geoff. "You'll frighten the herons." Fred bobbed down beside him, his pain forgotten.

"There's Great Crested Newts in the mere," he announced quietly. "I just seen 'em swimming near the bank over there." He pointed in the direction of his sighting.

"You sure?" queried Brian, putting down his binoculars.

"I'm bloody sure. Come and look." The other two looked at each other and then scrambled out from the reed bed. Following Fred along the bank to the stream, they arrived at the spot and looked down into the water. The newts obligingly flashed their undersides.

"Oh my God! You're right, Fred. They're Great Crested Newts. We have to report this to Natural England cos they're a protected species," Geoff said.

"And you know what else, guys? Those effing planners won't be allowed to build around here unless they get a special licence, and I bet they won't get a licence because of what they want to do to the land!"

***

As soon as he got home, he told Lorraine who immediately phoned Mandy.

"That's bloody fantastic news, Lorraine!"

"What do you want to do next?"

"I'm going to phone Terry Bailey right now and let him know. Could Brian please put this all on-line, and I'll WhatsApp everyone, too."

"Will do, Mandy."

***

The Stonechester Gazette banner headline screamed, 'Have I got Newts for You' with a Terry Bailey by-line.

Fred Denton could feel himself blanch as he read the front page. He phoned Douglas.

"Have you read today's Stonechester Gazette, Doug?"

"I only read the Financial Times, Fred." His contemptuous tone riled Fred.

"You ought to bloody read it. Because we are now well and truly screwed!" Douglas's tone was sharp.

"What do you mean?" Fred told him. There was silence at the other end. Then, "Do you mean to say that we can't go ahead with the application because of a load of fucking tadpoles?"

"Yes." There was silence again. It went on for so long that Fred asked, "You still there?" A deep sigh answered him, then, "The lockdown has been lifted. When are the next council meetings?"

"Next week. Stonechester's on Tuesday and Norssex on Thursday."

"Right. Fred, you're going to have to really push this lot through and fast. My backers won't wait now that lockdown is over. This all hangs on you being able to get the application OK'd, otherwise we all go down together, and we can kiss our millions goodbye."

Fred sat down heavily, sweating. This was going to take a miracle.

***

The following Friday, an Extraordinary General Meeting of the PVP was held in St Agatha's. The church was brimming with people. Reverend Michael and Barbera Fuller were delighted to see the pews full again, although saddened by the loss of so many due to Covid.

Barbera was feeling a lot better nowadays but still suffered from bouts of fatigue and shortness of breath. There were so many volunteers in the church nowadays that she didn't need to worry about the tea urns, drinks or biscuits. It was so nice to relax and not stress.

Lady Caroline ascended to the pulpit, the stairs creaking under her weight. Sir Henry sat in the front pew, this time on his own. He felt that it would politic if that nice lady from the yoga class sat with her group. Perhaps, he could persuade Caroline to play more golf...

"Ladies and gentlemen, your attention please!" Lady Caroline. People began shushing each other until there was silence.

"First of all, welcome back. Lockdown is over but do let us remember those who, most unfortunately, succumbed to Covid. I would like to hold a two-minute silence in their memory. Please stand."

Everyone stood. There was absolute silence for two minutes. Then everyone sat down. Lady Caroline continued, "I would ask Mrs Culverhouse and Mrs Sharman to bring us all up to speed. There's good news, I believe."

Mandy and Rita stood in the middle aisle.

"You go, first," whispered Rita. Mandy gave a quick nod.

"There is some very good news. The application for outline planning permission had been deferred by both the Norssex and Stonechester councils. This was helped by the discovery of an endangered species by members of the Stonechester Twitchers and Birders Club and also the discovery of what is thought to be a Saxon dwelling of some kind by members of the Stonechester Historical Society. Congratulations and thanks to those societies." There was a spontaneous burst of applause. Mandy waited until the clapping had stopped.

"However, the application is still only deferred. It hasn't gone away. The Great Crested Newts could be moved to another lake and once Historical England has excavated the site, we may well be back to square one. I, therefore, suggest we maintain our objections to the Pyddel Valley and wold undergoing any kind of development." There was a lot of here, here's and nods of agreement. Mandy nudged Rita and hissed, "Your turn."

Rita spoke, "Ladies and gentlemen, we, therefore, propose that the PVP takes our campaign one step further. Our proposal is that we hold a demonstration to show the powers that be we will not see our wonderful countryside disappear under concrete and tarmac." She had learnt the words by rote but spoke them from her heart. Their impact was almost instantaneous. The whole church broke into applause.

Somebody called out, "When?"

When the applause had died down, Mandy spoke, "We propose that we hold it on Sunday, 4th April which is Easter Sunday. Reverend Fuller has kindly agreed that we meet here at St Agatha's and, after a brief service, make our way along the Pyddel Valley and up onto the wold, then to the Saxon ruins and the mere so that he can make a blessing at each place." There was another round of applause.

Rita took over, "Please talk about us. Tell people about our protest. We want to show the councils that we say no to any kind of envelopment." Everyone clapped her, ignoring her verbal faux pas. They all knew what she meant. She blushed. She couldn't believe that she could speak like that. Mandy gave her a hug. Reverend Fuller now stepped forward.

"Ladies and gentlemen. I would invite you all to join me in a prayer for love, peace and compassion." Everyone stood as he intoned some deeply felt words, and there was a loud, collective amen. Even Lady Caroline forgot to bluster from the pulpit and quietly descended, apart from the odd creak, to join the people leaving the church.

April, 2021

"Well, well, well, Greg. Our Douglas must be shitting himself." Her black eyes were twinkling with gallows humour, and she was grinning from ear to ear. He couldn't help but join her in smiling.

"You couldn't make it up, could you?" he opined. "I mean, really. A Saxon church and burial site and what have you, and some big yellow tadpoles with tails. Christ, whatever next?"

"According to their *Facebook* page and website, they're going to organise a big demonstration to show the local councils that development of any kind is a no–no. On Easter Sunday. That's this weekend. I think a trip up there is in order. Coming?"

"Yes, OK." He was surprised at himself for agreeing to go but he could stay with Yvonne, the Russell, Harding receptionist, for a couple of days. He made a mental note to give her a ring.

"Eleven o'clock, St Agatha's, this Sunday. I'll see you then. Oh, by the way, the director has agreed that the SFO can sequester the Holmes bank account. I briefed him thus far, but he wants more evidence, especially regarding Russell, Harding and money laundering." Greg nodded.

"Hopefully, that won't be too much longer. They must all be running scared."

***

As soon as Boris Johnson had informed the nation that the third lockdown was over, Historical England had contacted the Norssex Finds Liaison Office and the County Coroner. A meeting was arranged for two of their senior archaeologists, Joe and Bob, to meet up with Clare, June and Susan at the site. They were accompanied by Harry Baines, the County Finds Officer.

On arrival at the site, accompanied by Harry, Bob began to carry out a geo-physical survey with something that looked like a TV aerial.

"It's just like *Time Team,*" breathed Susan excitedly. They were watching the other archaeologist, Joe, as he gently dug away more turf and soil from the wall that the ladies had discovered. The silence was so intense. Suddenly, he looked up at them.

"Wow! We've got some stonework here, possibly Roman. I think we may have the foundations of a Saxon church."

"Isn't that unusual?" asked Clare. "They usually built in wood, didn't they?"

"You're quite right, Mrs Capps." He nodded at her appreciatively. "Sometimes, though, if they found any stones that the Romans had built their forts with, they'd utilise them for a church." He pointed out across the valley with his trowel.

"You'd be able to see it for miles. We will have to see if the geo-phys confirms the foundations of a Saxon round tower church. It may also have been used as a lookout for any Viking long boats coming up the Pyddel."

"Surely, the Pyddel is too shallow for a long boat?" June said.

"You'd be surprised, Mrs Packwood. Viking long boats had very shallow draughts. Besides, the Pyddel was probably a lot broader and deeper in those days. Later, agriculture and land drainage have made it the width it is today probably."

Harry had returned with Bob.

"We've definitely got a really, really interesting site, Joe," he said. Harry nodded. "It's almost certainly late Saxon. The place name ending in 'ham' is a bit of a give-away, isn't it?" Seeing June look a bit mystified, he clarified. "Place names with a suffix of 'ham' indicate a Saxon village or settlement."

"Yep," Bob agreed. "We need to get a full team up here to do an in-depth excavation."

"I'm up for that," said Joe. He got up and smiled at them. "A few trenches won't be enough to do it justice. Honestly, ladies, you've discovered a site of tremendous historical interest. There's probably a cemetery here, too." Turning to Harry and Bob, he said, "Let's get back to the office. I want to have a look at the geo-phys results."

Both archaeologists packed up their gear and followed the ladies and Harry back down the path into the Pyddel Valley.

"It's really nice here," said Joe as they trudged along the bank.

"Yes, it is," agreed Susan. "That's why we don't want anybody building warehouses up on the wold, where we've just been, or roads down here."

"You're joking!" exploded Bob. "It's lovely, even on a cloudy day like this. The view across the valley, from where we were, was gorgeous."

"Glad you think so," said June. They had now arrived in back in Lower Pyddelham.

"Thank you, ladies. It's been a pleasure." Bob shook their hands, followed by Joe and Harry. "We'll be in touch shortly." With that, they loaded their equipment into a Land Rover and drove off followed by Harry in a Corsa.

"Well, what a wonderful day!" exclaimed Susan. "Do either of you fancy a drink in the Cat and Cradle? To celebrate, sort of."

"That's a great idea," agreed Clare. "Let's go."

***

Fred Denton was an extremely worried man. In fact, he was worried sick. He had tried very hard at both council meetings to get the application for outline planning permission through to the planning inspectorate. The plans had been studied in detail, the benefits of a supermarket, six warehouses and a solar panel farm offering local employment and clean, green energy had been discussed at length but to no avail. Fred put this down to the PVP, its *Facebook* and website, the recent discoveries, the on-line petition which had attracted over six thousand signatures and the publicity given by Terry Bailey's articles in the *Stonechester Gazette.*

He saw Terry, sitting in the public seating areas of both meeting venues, jotting away in a notebook. He tried to keep his face impassive, but he felt murderous. His blood pressure was through the roof, and he was drinking more than usual. He dreaded phoning Douglas, but he was more frightened of returning Christiana's call. She really scared him because she was so ruthless.

Deciding to bite the bullet of bad news, he sat in his BMW and rang Douglas after the Norssex County Council meeting.

"It's me, Doug."

"About bloody time. Well?"

"It's been deferred again because of all the stuff with the newts and Historical England."

There was silence at the other end.

"Look, Doug. It's been deferred not kicked out. We can get a licence and remove the newts and the excavation is only over a small area by that steep bit on the wold. We'll just have to wait a bit longer."

"My investors won't wait. Al-defidel Supermarkets won't wait either; they'll just look elsewhere if the warehousing doesn't happen." Douglas's voice was flat without emotion. Fred wondered if he had also been drinking a lot, too.

"Have you heard from Sonia?"

"Yes. She texted me. She wants £500,000 otherwise she's going to the cops. She's not interested in me leaving

Eve now. She doesn't even want to talk to me. She knows that I'm probably going to be the next Stonechester MP. She just wants money."

"What are we going to do?"

"Well, we haven't got that sort of money to pay her off. I told you that."

"Would you like me and Christiana to have a word with her. We might be able to do a deal?"

"Do what you like."

"Can you give her number then. Please." Douglas texted him with the information. "Got it. Thanks." Changing the subject, Fred asked, "When is the election of the next Stonechester MP being held?"

"I'm on the shortlist. It's the final selection, and I have to give a speech at the special general meeting being held on the Friday after Easter. Eve's writing my script. It's between me, Maud Henderson and Ronit Patel."

"Edna and I will be voting for you, Doug, you can rest assured."

"Gee thanks." Douglas's sarcasm raised Fred's blood pressure another few points. He was dying for a glass of Chivas.

"Well, we can't do much more until after Easter, Doug. Concentrate on getting yourself elected the Conservative MP for Stonechester." Douglas didn't bother answering; Fred saw his call terminated. You bastard, he thought.

***

"It's me, Christiana. We've got a problem."

"Nothing new there, Fred."

"Let's meet at the usual place. Can you make it today? We need to sort this before the Easter break."

"OK. I can do 6:00 p.m."

"Good. See you then."

***

Easter Sunday at St Agatha's. Lower Pyddelham was heaving. Cars were parked bumper to bumper all around the village. The church was full but people were still trying to squeeze themselves into the pews or stand at the back.

Bang on 11:00 a.m., Reverend Fuller began his Easter service. He had decided to keep it as brief as possible, as he had anticipated a large crowd and was worried about health and safety. Between the Stonechester Gazette, the Norbrough Chronicle and the PVP's Facebook page and website, today's event had been widely communicated to one and all; it looked like the whole of Norssex had turned up.

Once the service was over, Reverend Fuller led the way out of St Agatha's, along the Pyddel Valley and up onto the wold. Reaching the top, he looked back down and was amazed at the number of people making their way to join him. Whilst waiting, he glanced around and saw a police car and a BBC Outlook East Midlands van parked beside the hedge. There was also a hotdog van parked further along the path. Reverend Fuller tutted to himself.

Even on a solemn day like today, there was always someone who wanted to make money.

Most of the crowd had now joined him, many with banners; the destruction of the countryside and the evils of industrial development were their main themes. The BBC cameraman and soundman followed in their wake, filming the scene and a young reporter was stopping people and interviewing them.

Reverend Fuller thanked those nearest for attending and began to bless the Pyddel Valley. Then he led them on a longish walk to the mere where, again, he blessed the newts and all wildlife. He saw the BBC team had followed them.

Historical England had already begun its excavations and these had been roped off to protect them during the Easter break. Reverend Fuller stopped and blessed the area in memory of the Saxons and anyone else who may have worshipped and been buried on this site. For a few moments, everyone in the crowd was silent, struck by the scenery below them: the sun had suddenly emerged from behind a candyfloss of cloud, and its light was softly embracing the land right to the horizon. The new, fresh greens of spring, the pale blue sky, the sunlight twinkling on the river itself and the tiny villages and scattered farm buildings below them made the scene ethereal.

"May the Lord God bless this land and keep it safe for evermore," intoned Reverend Fuller. There was a loud chorus of 'amen'.

"Ladies, gentlemen and children," he shouted. There were so many people. "Thank you all for coming here today in support of our protest against the proposed development up here on the wold and down in the valley. We really do appreciate it." There was a burst of applause and some cheering.

"Please continue to enjoy this wonderful countryside, but I would respectfully ask that you take your litter home with you. Thank you."

The crowd began breaking up but not before posing in front of the cameraman. Most people volunteered themselves to be interviewed before making their way back down the path into the valley and their cars, but a few small groups had wandered off or were making their way to the hotdog van.

"Reverend Fuller, may I interview you?" This was from the young, ingenuous-looking BBC reporter.

"I'd rather not, sir," he replied. "I think it's best you speak with Mrs Culverhouse and/or Mrs Sharman of the Stonechester and District Wellbeing Walkers Club as they have been the leading lights in our protest."

"Where would I find these ladies, Reverend?"

"We're right here." Mandy and Rita stepped forward. The interview began.

Meanwhile, Sergeant Kenneth Dunkley was sitting in the police car, observing the scenes unfolding before him with rather a jaundiced eye. After nearly thirty-five years of service in the Stonechester force, he knew the land and its populace like the back of his hand. He was bored stiff and passed the time by giving a running but un-PC commentary to the newest recruit to the Stonechester

Constabulary. Constable Reepok Patel, sitting in the passenger seat, was feeling very uncomfortable.

"I see Bert Cowdrey is already here," Sergeant Dunkley said, nodding in direction of the hotdog van. "He's always got an eye for the main chance. Any chance of making a few bob, that is, even on a religious day like today." Constable Patel commented that a queue was already forming for Bert's food and drink.

"They'll all end up with salmonella if they eat his stuff," was Sergeant Dunkley's curt reply. As the banners came closer, he remarked, "Here come the WaNKers and the PRaTs."

"What do you mean, Sarge?" asked Constable Patel, horrified at his language. His Sergeant laughed.

"Women against Nature Killers and Pyddleham Riders against Tyranny. Look over there!" He pointed at another clutch of banners just coming into view. These were being carried by members of Weight Watchers and Slimmer's World." He chuckled.

"It's the Battle of the Bulges!" he guffawed. "It'll be bathroom scales at dawn." Constable Patel did not share his Sergeant's puerile sense of humour. In fact, he was quite shocked and hoped that the demonstration wouldn't last too long so that they could return to the station and he could go off duty. He found Ken Dunkley totally repulsive. Oblivious to his Constable's dislike, the Sergeant continued his commentary.

"Look, a witch invasion!" He pointed to four women holding up a very large banner in front of the BBC cameraman, chanting, "No warehouses, no developments." A very tall woman, with dreadlocks and dressed from head to foot in purple, suddenly broke into, "We shall overcome." Sergeant Dunkley tutted.

"It's that Cassandra Harrison and her lot," he informed Constable Patel. "She's a real weirdo, her. A couple of years ago, she advertised in the *Stonechester Gazette* for twelve virgins to help her in purifying the land in and around the town but only three turned up." He looked at the four, now standing in a circle, chanting. "You can see why they're still virgins." He began laughing. Constable Patel regarded him with disgust. He decided enough was enough, and he began to get out of the police car. Suddenly, there was some loud screaming. A woman came running towards them. Sergeant Dunkley wound down his window.

"What's the matter, madam?" She was short of breath from running and stuttered in her breathlessness.

"There–there–there's a body. A w-w-woman. C-come please." Sergeant Dunkley began to manoeuvre his bulk from the driver's seat but Constable Patel was already following the woman towards the mere. Swearing under his breath, Sergeant Dunkley puffed along behind them through the small groups of people who were now converging into a crowd.

"Sarge, look!" exclaimed Constable Patel. As the Sergeant neared a small reed bed and bent down, he saw the body. It lay prone, almost submerged in the water, the reeds around it bent and broken. It had been well hidden. "Jesus," he said. He stood upright. "Right, Constable Patel. Let's get everyone away from here. I'll ring for back-up." Inwardly, he was annoyed. It was going to be a long old day.

***

"Good evening, and welcome to Outlook East Midlands this Easter Monday. We wish all viewers a very happy Easter," the female presenter purred, staring glassy-eyed into the camera. She wished she hadn't drunk anything at lunch. It had been one G and T too far. Her male colleague took up the dialogue, trying not to look directly at the auto-prompt in front of them. "First, tonight, a report on the Pyddelham Valley Protest demonstration held yesterday which has led to police finding a body. Full details coming up. Second, can Lupton Town Football Club make it to the Premier League? Ben James reports from their brand-new 'Come all ye Faithfull' stand. We also report on the latest from Stonechester where residents have been enjoying a resurgence in locally brewed ales but local police are concerned about their potential for causing anti-social behaviour." His female colleague, trying to focus on what appeared to be three auto-prompts, was wishing she could remove her contact lenses and dentures, but took over.

"But flurst, the Pyddelham Valley Protest. Here sour reporter, Ned Kelly, alive from Lower Pyddely. Led."

Fred Denton, watching the young and eager Ned reporting live on TV, was dying a thousand deaths. He could feel his heart pounding in his ears and the sweat trinkling down his back. The meeting he and Christiana had with Sonia Bailey would haunt him forever. He shot a quick look at Edna but she was concentrating on her knitting.

"Just going to make a call, Edna." She didn't answer so he slipped out and took his mobile into the conservatory. He pressed the call button.

"It's me. Have you seen the local news on the BBC?"

"Yeah. Do you know who it is?" asked Douglas. Fred decided to play dumb.

"No. The cops haven't released any details yet."

"Well, that's us all totally fucked. My investors and Aldefidel won't want to know now. First it's a Saxon church, then some overgrown tadpoles and now a bloody murder." Douglas sighed. "Fred, I'm bankrupt. No money left. Zilch. Nada." If it was possible, Fred felt his blood pressure rise another couple of points. Douglas continued, "I don't know what I'm going to do."

***

Easter Monday morning in Cockspur Street and a meeting was in progress. Greg was there, along with Detective Chief Inspector Alan Gordon of the Stonechester Police, Detective Chief Superintendent Billy Grey of the Norssex County Police and various other people who the lady with the black eyes did not introduce. She began the meeting in her usual no-nonsense manner.

"Right, DCI Gordon. Who was she?" He shuffled his copy of the post mortem report.

"She was Sonia Elaine Bailey, aged twenty-nine, living in a flat in Norbrough, and employed as an assistant in a company of investment consultants in London. Her next of kin is her brother, Terry Bailey, a reporter with the *Stonechester Gazette*. According to the PM, there was blunt force trauma to the back of the head but that would've only stunned her although there would've been some bleeding. It was a stab wound in her left ribcage that actually killed her. Whatever it was, went right into her heart and, interestingly, the person who did it is likely to be left-handed so had to be standing behind her when the blow was delivered. When she was found, she'd been dead about forty-eight hours."

"Was it a knife of some kind?" asked DCS Grey. DCI Gordon shook his head.

"No, the Pathologist reckons it was something long and thin, a bit like a stiletto but flatter with sharp sides. He also said that she wasn't killed where she was found. There were some carpet fibres on her skirt."

"Dumped in the mere post mortem then." DCI Gordon nodded.

"Any tyre tracks?"

"There may well have been but that demo they had yesterday has basically destroyed any."

"Do we know anything else about her?" asked DCS Grey. Greg quickly looked at the woman with the black eyes who nodded slightly.

"She's the mistress, or was, of Douglas Antony Yardley-Henderson. We know that he has been laundering money for the Russians and Albanians OCGs through various shell companies in land deals, hitherto with some success. However, luckily for us, his latest venture into warehousing and solar panel farm development in the Pyddelhams and surrounding area has been his downfall." Greg looked around at their faces; he had their complete attention. "I have to be honest and say that's due mainly to the locals who have put up quite a fight." The lady with the black eyes took up the dialogue.

"Greg is quite right. The locals don't realise it but their activities have helped us enormously. We've been watching Yardley-Henderson for a few years now. He's not alone. We have evidence to show that one of the local councillors is also involved. Fred Denton is on the Norssex County Council and is Leader of the Stonechester Borough Council. He is very fond of gambling and has run up quite a lot of debt from time to time. Greg, please continue."

"Thank you, ma'am." Greg looked around at the meeting. "As well as being paid off by Yardley-Henderson for insider information about land and council affairs, Denton has a contact in a firm of solicitors in Stonechester called Harding, Russell. My own contact there tells me that she and the other secretaries are aware that some of the deals made by the firm might not be the right side of legal. In particular, there's talk about Senior Probate Manager, Christiana Morleigh, and a conveyancing manager called Jeremy Fisher. They say that these two seem to work very closely together." He took a sip of water from the glass at his elbow.

"So, gentlemen, it is our intention to apply for search warrants for the offices of Harding, Russell as well as the homes of Messrs Yardley-Henderson, Denton, Fisher and Miss Morleigh."

"Do you think we'll find anything conclusive?" asked DCS Grey. The lady with the black eyes nodded.

"Oh yes, I believe we will." She gave an unpleasant smile "We have written and verbal evidence from a Felicity Holmes who became involved with Harding, Russell owing to the death of her uncle. We also have evidence of malpractice given to us by other clients of this firm. Gentlemen, I firmly believe we will succeed in obtaining substantial prison sentences for those people I have mentioned. I also firmly believe that one, or more, of them are guilty of the murder of Sonia Bailey." DCI Gordon stood up.

"Right," he said. "Let's get cracking."

***

"Poor Terry was in tears," reported Rita to Mandy and Lorraine. "I brought him back here for a couple of stiff drinks after he'd identified her body."

"Poor guy," said Lorraine. "Good thing you were with him, Rita."

"Well, there's no other family and we've known the Baileys for donkeys. It's the least Len and me could do."

"When's the funeral?" asked Mandy.

"Reverend Fuller said he'd do it once the body is released by the coroner. So, it's just waiting for that."

Mandy said, "Let's drink a toast to Sonia Bailey as I think her murder may be the final thing that stops the development."

"Here, here," agreed Rita. "To Sonia Bailey. God bless her."

"To Sonia," they both repeated and clinked glasses.

***

The police raids on the offices of Harding, Russell, the homes of the Yardley-Hendersons and the Dentons, as well as those of Christiana Morleigh and Jeremy Fisher, took place simultaneously a week later. At nine o'clock in the morning on the Friday after Easter.

At the offices of Harding, Russell laptops and computers were put into plastic bags to go away for analyses. Forensic accountants from the SFO took over the offices and began to go through client files and accounts. All staff were sent home with exception of Christiana Morleigh and Jeremy Fisher who were taken to Norbrough police station for questioning. They were soon joined by Douglas and Fred, the former objecting loudly and demanding his rights to a lawyer.

"Let's let them sweat for an hour or so and then we'll start the questioning," suggested the lady with the black eyes. She was watching Douglas Yardley-Henderson through the glass observation window as he paced the room. "What's Denton doing?"

"He's sitting down and sobbing," said Greg. "Morleigh and Fisher are just sitting quietly in their rooms."

"Excuse me," a young constable interrupted them. "I've got a Mrs Edna Denton asking to speak to the person in charge."

"Right. Thank you." She turned to Greg. "You can come with me. This should be interesting."

They followed the young Constable into a pleasant room where Edna Denton had made herself comfortable in one of the armchairs.

"Mrs Denton, good morning. My name is Carol Sharpe and I work for the Serious Fraud Office. This is my colleague, Greg Williamson, who works for the National Crime Agency. Do you mind if we ask a senior police officer to join us?"

"No, of course not. The more, the merrier." In fact, Edna Denton did look extremely merry; it was as if she had shed her innocuous appearance and had come alive.

"Greg, could you ask Detective Chief Inspector Gordon to join us." Greg disappeared, returning a few moments later with DCI Gordon and DCS Grey. When they were all sitting down, Carol said, "How may we help you, Mrs Denton?"

"Oh no, it's me helping you. I've quite a bit to tell you about Fred but first things first. Here's his laptop that your men missed because he hid it under the floorboards in his bedroom, and you may wish to check out our loft because I know there are things up there that Fred wouldn't like the world to know about." Edna leaned back into her armchair looking very pleased with herself.

"Er, right. DCI Gordon, may I ask you to organise a search of the loft and perhaps you'd be kind enough to pass this laptop on for analysis. Thank you so much." He took the laptop, placed it in a large evidence bag and disappeared through the door. He returned in time to hear – "Mrs Denton, do you mind if we record what you are about to say?" asked DCS Grey.

"Not at all. Please do but could I be cheeky and have a nice pot of tea and some biscuits while I talk? Chocolate digestives would be lovely. I've a lot to tell you and my mouth does tend to become dry."

***

"Jesus," exclaimed Greg. It was late afternoon and they were looking at the results the IT boffins had got from Fred Denton's secret loft laptop. "He's a fucking paedo."

"As well as lots of other things besides," said DCS Grey. "He's been stupid enough to keep his "accounts" in Excel and there are a couple of incriminating documents he's saved in Word. How thick can you get!"

"I suppose he thought he'd never be found out," opined DCI Gordon.

"To be honest, all the evidence came from his wife," said Greg. "One bastard down, three to go." As an afterthought, he added, "She must really hate him." The others nodded.

"Where's your SFO lady?" asked DCS Grey.

"She's about to watch the Christiana Morleigh interview. Let's join her."

***

The police raid on Christiana Morley's three bedroomed house in a highly desirable area of Norbrough had produced a laptop, a mobile phone and a USB flash drive. These were all analysed, the results of which were presented to Carol Sharpe and the others.

"Well, well, well. Blackmail too. She's versatile if nothing else. No wonder Fred is sobbing. I reckon Douglas will be sobbing too." She grinned. "DCS Grey, do you mind if I join you and DCI Gordon in this interview? They both looked at each other."

"It's not usual but, yeah, please join us," agreed the DCS.

"Thank you. Her solicitor's here so let's get started." Greg watched them through the observation window as they entered the room where Christiana and a man sat in deep discussion. Once seated DCS Grey switched on the recording machine and introduced themselves. Christiana looked simultaneously defiant and contemptuous.

"Miss Morleigh, you've been brought here to help with our enquiries with regard to international money laundering, fraud and perverting the course of justice." She looked at the three of them and sneered.

"Really? I have no idea why I'm here. I have no idea why you have desecrated my home but I will be applying for compensation and an apology."

"Well let me enlighten you, Miss Morleigh." DCS Grey began to set out various documents in front of her and her solicitor as well as a mobile phone and a flash drive in plastic evidence bags. "First of all, here is a list of calls made from this mobile phone found in your home. You will see that quite a few are made to Fred Denton's and a couple to Jeremy Fisher's. You have also received calls from their mobiles, as the list shows."

"Jeremy and I work together at Russell, Harding and I know Fred Denton socially. So what?"

As Carol Sharpe's black eyes bored into her, she shifted slightly in her chair. DCS Grey pointed to another piece of paper.

"This is a bank statement from the ROT Bank. It's your bank?" She said nothing. Her solicitor spoke.

"It'd look better for you if you answered." She gave him a withering look.

"Yes, I bank with the ROT. So?"

"You've had a few credits over the years. Quite substantial sums. For example, just before Christmas, you received £10,000. Who was that from?"

"From Russell, Harding. A thank you bonus for our work during Covid."

"Right, right." DCI Gordon nodded. He continued, "Strange that because when we made enquiries with ROT, the money was transferred to you from an account in the Caymen Islands. It was the same for the other substantial amounts you have received over the past five or so years." She didn't answer, just stared at the paper he was pointing at. Her solicitor was making notes on his pad, his pen scratching away at the heavy silence. He pointed at another piece of paper.

"What is this one, DCI Gordon?"

"Miss Morleigh, we downloaded your flash drive. It proved very interesting. Why were you blackmailing Fred Denton?" She didn't move, continuing to stare at the paperwork on the table in front of her, aware of four pairs of eyes studying her.

"No comment." Carol Sharpe spoke.

"I'm from the Serious Fraud Office, Miss Morleigh. Or should I call you Miss Christine Muriel Mullen, born in Church Lane, Stonechester on 10th April, 1979?" Christiana looked up, her face white and her eyes blazing; suddenly half-standing she tried to throw a punch at Carol but her solicitor pulled her back into her chair.

"I think you've clearly demonstrated that I am correct. You attended Stonechester Secondary Modern and did quite well academically but then went a little off the rails. Amphetamines and LSD wasn't it. Dealing. You did time in Young Offenders, came out and got a typist job at Harding, Russell. How did you get where you are today, Chris? Sleep with one of the senior partners. Or all of them?" Christiana, furious, made another attempt to hit her but was again restrained by her solicitor.

"I think that is quite inappropriate, Ms Sharpe," he said.

"No, not really." Turning to Christiana again, she asked, "I noticed that you tried to hit me with your left hand. Are you left-handed?"

"Why do you want to know?"

"You'd be wise to answer, Miss Morleigh," advised her solicitor. She sighed and then glared at Carol.

"Yes, I am."

"Did you know Sonia Bailey?"

"Who's she? No."

"Do you know Douglas Yardley-Henderson?"

"I've heard of him. He's up for MP for Stonechester, I believe."

"How do you know that?"

"Fred must've told me."

"So, you've been in contact with Fred Denton."

"I bloody told you, I know him socially. I suppose he told me at some cocktail party we both went to."

"Not by text?"

"What? What the fuck do you mean?"

"What I mean is, Chris, we have got all the texts you have received and sent on your mobile. They really do make very interesting reading. You and Fred are as thick as thieves, and I use that phrase appropriately. You have been for years."

"No comment." Greg smiled inwardly as he and the two detectives watched the shark go in for the kill. Carol pointed at another piece of paper.

"One of the text conversations you had with him dated, let's see, on 1st April, how very appropriate by the way, indicates that Sonia was threatening to go to the police unless she received £500,000. Fred is saying Sonia's already turned down £50,000 and that there's no more money."

"No comment."

"Then you texted him on the morning of 2nd April. Your text says, *"Problem sorted."* What did you mean?"

"No comment."

"Does this belong to you?" She placed a plastic evidence bag on the table. In it was a long, flat silver letter opener.

"No comment."

"We found this in your office at Harding, Russell. Forensics have found traces of blood on it. The blood group is the same as Miss Sonia Bailey's. The carpet strands found on her skirt match exactly the carpet in the hallway outside your office." Greg inwardly thanked Yvonne, the receptionist, for telling him about the letter opener; she had been threatened with it by an irate Christiana when she had inadvertently cut off one of Christiana's clients during a very important phone call.

"Let me tell you what happened, Chris. You got Fred to call Sonia and invite her to your office after everyone had gone home on Thursday night for the Easter break. Did he tell her she was about to collect that £500,000? Well, whatever. She turns up, and you both invite her in to your office and you both try and persuade her to wait for her money. What happened next, Chris?"

"No comment."

"Well, Chris, I reckon she refused to wait and threatened you both with exposure. Douglas Yardley-Henderson probably told her everything in pillow talk. She was dangerous. Very dangerous. So, we know you stabbed her with this." Carol held up the evidence bag with the letter opener. "But did you hit her on the head or did Fred do that? My gut says it was you, Chris."

"No comment."

"We also went all over your car. You and Fred must've carried her body between you and put it in the boot because although you did a super cleaning job, Forensics managed to find some traces of blood. Again, Sonia Bailey's." There was absolute silence. Christiana glared at the three of them, murder in her eyes.

"No comment." Her solicitor sighed.

DCS Grey broke the silence.

"Christine Muriel Mullen, otherwise known as Christiana Morleigh, I am arresting you for the murder of Sonia Bailey on the evening of Thursday, 1st April this year, as well as for aiding and abetting fraud and international money laundering, and for perverting the course of justice. You do not have to say anything but it may harm your defence if you do not mention when questioned something which you later rely on in court. Anything you do say may be given in evidence. Do you wish to say anything else?" She glared at him. *Christ,* he thought, *if looks could kill.*

"No fucking comment."

***

"Right, let's interview Fred Denton next," Carol said. The three of them made their way to another interview room and entered. Fred was sitting next to his solicitor. He'd stopped crying and looked like a corpse. DCI Gordon introduced themselves for the benefit of the recording. If it was possible, Fred's pallor became greyer. He stared at the table in front of him.

"Now, Mr Denton, we've called you in to answer questions in connection with the murder of Miss Sonia Bailey. Did you know her?"

"Er, no."

"Well, Mr Denton, how do you account for the fact that when we checked your mobile, her number was on a list of calls." He took out a piece of paper from a file, placed it in front of Fred and his solicitor, and pointed to a highlighted mobile number. "There are also quite a few calls to and from Christiana Morleigh as well as Douglas Yardley-Henderson."

"Er, that call you said about was a mis-dial. A mistake."

"Then how do you account for the fact that you received a text from Douglas Yardley-Henderson with Miss Bailey's mobile number?" Fred continued to stare at the table but began to tremble.

"No c-comment," he stuttered.

"Where were you last Thursday evening?"

"At home. With my wife."

"Ah, that's also strange because Mrs Denton has told us that you left home at around 5:30 p.m. that evening and returned around 7:30 p.m. She also said you looked terrible, as if you'd had a nasty shock. Would you please tell us where you went." Fred was now visibly trembling.

"No comment. Can I have a glass of water please?" Carol Sharpe got up and went to the door asking the WPC outside to bring in a glass of water. When the glass was placed on the table in front of him, Fred picked it up, his hand shaking so badly that he spilt some of its contents.

"Can my client have a break please," the solicitor asked.

"Of course. We'll be back in ten minutes." The three left the room and took the opportunity to have a coffee break themselves. Carol said, "he's ready to spill the beans. May I question him on the fraud and then you can take over with the murder and the porno."

"Yes, I've no problems with that," replied DCS Grey. "After him, I suggest we interview Fisher. That shouldn't take too long. Then Yardley-Henderson. Agreed?"

"Agreed," the others echoed him.

"Right, his ten minutes is up. Let's go back."

Back in the room, Fred had managed to get some self-control back. Greg had watched him through the observation window whilst his solicitor gave him a talking-to. Carol Sharpe began the questioning.

"Mr Denton, I work for the Serious Fraud Office and I'm here because we have evidence that you have abused your position as a councillor by acting as a link for Douglas Yardley-Henderson and Christiana Morleigh in that you have passed on highly sensitive information for payment regarding land sales and purchases that, as you know well, are covers for international money laundering."

"No co-comment."

"Where is your evidence, Miss Sharpe," the solicitor asked.

"Here." With that, she produced a laptop, a mobile and a wad of bank statements.

"These belong to you, Mr Denton?" she asked.

"Er, yes. Er, I mean no comment."

"Your wife was most helpful. She gave us the passwords. When our IT guys investigated, we found spreadsheets with financial data which correlated to these bank statements from two banks in the Channel Islands. You have also received substantial payments from the Caymen Islands. How do you account for that?"

"No, no comment."

"Mr Denton, we have evidence from your mobile and your laptop that you have been involved in assisting Douglas Yardley-Henderson in money laundering. You will therefore be charged with fraud and assisting an offender in international money laundering. I am now leaving the room at 13.23. DCS Grey and DCI Gordon will now conduct the rest of this interview." She got up and left the room, joining Greg on the other side of the observation window.

"Mr Denton, we also found another laptop in the loft. When we investigated its contents, we found child pornography downloaded from the dark web. Your wife told us that nobody goes into the loft, only you. Do you have anything to say?" Fred was now shaking from head to foot; he couldn't speak. His solicitor was looking at him in disgust.

"You will be charged with downloading indecent images of children under current legislation at the end of this interview, Mr Denton. Before we do that, we would like to ask you more questions about the murder of Miss Sonia Bailey. Where did you go last Thursday evening?"

***

The discovery of his "porno" laptop was the last straw for Fred Denton. He began crying and in between sobs, told the detectives everything he knew about the money laundering operation, Christiana Morleigh and Russell, Harding and, of course, all about Douglas Yardley-Henderson.

"I didn't kill Sonia." He sobbed. "Honestly, I didn't. Christiana did it. Sonia came to the Russell, Harding offices at 6:00 p.m. on that Thursday as we'd arranged. She thought she was going to get her money cos I had told her that she would. Christiana and I tried to persuade her to wait for the money and I even offered fifty grand of my own to keep her sweet. She refused. She said she'd had enough of Doug and his promises to divorce Eve. She said she knew that once he was voted in as MP, she'd always just be his mistress whilst he and Eve would be rolling in money once the Outline Planning Permission had been granted. She said she deserved the money because she'd been buggered around by Doug. She said if we didn't pay her the half million by the end of next week, she'd go to you lot." He took in a deep breath and continued, "She got up and went to open the office door to leave but Christiana picked up a reading lamp and hit her on the back of the head. She began to stagger forwards onto the door itself but Christiana got a letter opener, came up behind her and stabbed her. I just stood there. I couldn't move." He began gulping and sobbing. "I swear I didn't kill her."

"What happened next, Mr Denton?" asked DCI Gordon.

"She'd slid down the door onto the carpet. We had to move her to open the door. Then Christiana told me to get her legs and I pulled her into the corridor whilst Christiana got her coat and handbag. Then we picked her up between us and carried her out the back entrance where her, Christiana's I mean, car was. We put her in the boot. Christiana told me to go home and that she would clean up. Nobody would ever know what had happened and she would get rid of the body."

"Did you go home?" Fred nodded. DCS Grey sighed. "Frederick Arthur Denton, I am charging you with being an accomplice to the murder of Miss Sonia Elaine Bailey on the evening of Thursday, 1st April this year, for aiding and abetting in international money laundering, to downloading child pornography from the dark web in contravention of…"

***

Jeremy Fisher was sitting patiently with his solicitor when the detectives and Carol Sharpe entered the room. His interview didn't take very long. He knew Christiana had been arrested too and once he had been shown his bank statements detailing the large sums of money received from the Cayman Islands, he decided to come clean and tell them everything he knew. DCI Gordon charged him with fraud, assisting in money laundering and perverting the course of justice.

***

It was now just after four o'clock when they entered the room where Douglas Yardley-Henderson was pacing up and down, complaining bitterly to his solicitor, Ambrose Cowley-Whyte.

"Good afternoon, Mr Yardley-Henderson," DCS Grey greeted them both with a small smile.

"About bloody time! I've been here since ten o'clock this morning, and I want to go home. Turning to his solicitor, he said, "Ambrose, you bloody read them my rights. What about habeus corpus?"

"For God's sake, calm down, Doug. And sit down. Now." Ambrose drew back the chair beside him. Douglas sat down reluctantly and regarded the three facing him, his face ugly. DCS Grey introduced themselves and apologised for keeping them both for so long. He started the interview.

"Do you know Jeremy Fisher?"

"Never heard of him. Oh, sorry, yes, I have. He's that frog Beatrix Potter wrote about, isn't he?" Douglas chuckled at his own joke but stopped when he noticed Carol Sharpe's black eyes regarding him with a look of utter contempt.

"Do you know Jeremy Fisher?" repeated DCS Grey.

"No, I've never heard of him."

"Do you know a Christiana Morleigh?"

"No, I've never heard of her."

"Do you know Fred Denton?"

"Yes, I know Fred. And his wife. Fred's a councillor and is also on the Stonechester Conservative Party Committee. Eve, my wife, and myself have met them loads of times at social events and so forth, especially as my name has been put forward in the election for the next Stonechester MP." DCI Gordon raised an eyebrow and took over the questioning.

"Do you know Felicity Holmes?"

"No, never heard of her."

"Well, this is all very odd, Douglas," remarked Carol Sharpe. "I hope you don't mind me calling you Douglas."

"I do, actually." Greg, behind the observation window, grinned to himself. *She won't like that,* he thought.

"Very well, Mr Yardley-Henderson. I'll come straight to the point. The Serious Fraud Office has been taking quite an interest in your business dealings over the past few years. We've noticed several interesting payments being credited to and debited from your business accounts, mainly from what have turned out to be shell companies. We've also noticed a couple of business trips to Tirana, in Albania, and also to Moscow. There have also been two trips to the Cayman Islands. You surely have got around."

"They are all legitimate business trips. Where's your proof anyway."

"Right here, Mr Yardley-Henderson." She fished out a large, thick file from her briefcase and placed various documents in front of Douglas and Ambrose. They viewed them with concern.

"Following those trips, several large amounts of money were credited to your account, which were then transferred to an account in Jersey. Why?"

"No comment."

"You denied knowing Felicity Holmes but, in fact, you and Fred Denton met her at her uncle's funeral and enquired if she was willing to sell his land since she was sole beneficiary. How did you know she was the sole beneficiary?" Douglas saw Ambrose shake his head slightly.

"No comment."

"We believe that Christiana Morleigh, Probate Manager at Harding, Russell, told Fred who told you. In fact, we know that she has passed on lots of information about Harding, Russell clients to you via Fred Denton. For example, information about the fact that Chris Tilley was looking to sell his land and change his will. I have a transcript of a recorded conversation we had with Miss Holmes before she died of Covid." She placed a three-page document in front of them. "She states that Jeremy Fisher passed on an offer for the Drage land from a company called DAYH Investments which she accepted. The money was transferred from a Cayman Island account. Mr Fisher has told us that Christiana Morleigh had told him to contact Miss Holmes with the offer from this company. So how did she, Christiana, get the information?"

"No comment." Douglas was now looking worried. Carol could see the beads of sweat on his upper lip.

"Mr Yardley-Henderson, I have to tell you that this file" – she tapped it – "contains incontrovertible proof that you and Fred Denton have been actively involved in international money laundering for the past five years or so. You have been using that money to buy up land and property. He has already told us in great detail about your activities in this field, especially with regard to the sale of the Tilley and Drage lands. Who are your so-called investors? Are they Albanian or Russian organised crime gangs?" Douglas was whey-faced and sweating heavily now. Ambrose looked at him.

"You don't have to answer, Doug."

"No comment."

"Can I ask for a break in the proceedings, DCS Grey. My client and I need to confer."

"I've finished my questioning," said Carol. "For now."

"We'll resume in twenty minutes," DCS Grey informed them. They left the room and went to join Greg by the observation window.

"He's really worried now," Greg observed. "So's his brief."

"Let's go for the jugular and question him about Sonia Bailey," said DCS Grey. "I'd like to get him charged today. Agreed?" They all nodded. "Coffee first, though."

Twenty minutes later, they were back. Douglas was looking a bit calmer. DCI Gordon took up the questioning.

"Do you know Sonia Bailey?" Douglas shot Ambrose a quick look. There was a very slight nod in response.

"Yes, I do. I mean, I did."

"In what capacity?"

"She was my mistress." Douglas shifted uncomfortably in his chair, aware of Carol's black eyes, watching his every move.

"Did your wife know about her?"

"Yes."

"Was your relationship with Sonia amicable, friendly?"

"For God's sake, she was my mistress. Of course, we were bloody friendly. Give me a break!"

"Well apparently not, of late. You were both seen in the Good Days coffee shop, Meeting Lane, Stonechester having a blazing argument a few weeks ago. There are dozens of witnesses who saw her pour coffee all over you."

"That was just a lovers' tiff."

"According to the witnesses at the next table, you told her you wouldn't be leaving your wife, at which point she stormed out of the shop. When did you see her again?"

"No comment."

"Did you see her again?"

"No comment."

"Well according to your mobile phone records, you were in contact with her quite a bit. Did she threaten you? Did she say she didn't want you any longer? Did she ask for hush money?"

"No comment."

"Did you inform Fred Denton what had happened?"

"No comment." DCS Grey interrupted.

"Mr Yardley-Henderson, all this 'no comment' is rather boring. You might as well know that Fred Denton has told us everything, and I do mean everything. We have transcripts of texts and e-mails and call lists for all your mobiles. We know you told him to go ahead and have a word with Sonia and texted him with her mobile number. How you—"

"Oh no. You're not bloody putting her murder on me! I had absolutely nothing to do with that." He looked mutinous. "Yes, all right, she threatened me. She knew I stood a good chance of being elected the next Stonechester MP and that I wouldn't leave Eve as this would jeopardise that. She demanded money, money I didn't have."

"Not until planning permission had been granted for all those warehouses, solar panel farm and supermarket," interrupted Carol. "Am I right?"

"No comment."

"Did you kill Sonia Bailey?"

Douglas jumped up and leaned across the table. The others managed to prevent him hitting her. He was breathing heavily when he sat down and answered. "No, I fucking didn't. I had absolutely nothing to do with it. Fred and Christiana were supposed to try and persuade her to wait," he sneered. "Looks like they failed."

"But you knew they were going to meet with her." The triumph in her black eyes was not lost on him.

"No comment." There was silence. Ambrose sighed heavily and leaned back in his chair as DCS Grey leaned forwards in his.

"Douglas Alexander Yardley-Henderson, I am charging you with being an accessory to the murder of Sonia Elaine Bailey on the evening of Thursday, 1st April, this year, for instigating, aiding and abetting in international money laundering, for perverting the course of justice. Anything you say…"

Ambrose Cowley-Whyte looked heavenwards. He wished he had never heard of Douglas Yardley-Henderson.

***

Edna Denton sat in her favourite armchair, knitting, with a large glass of Chivas Regal on a table beside her. Normally, she didn't drink the stuff but why waste it. Out of curiosity, she had phoned Norbrough police station to be told that her husband had been charged with various offences and that bail was unlikely. She was delighted with that news and was looking forward to her new-found freedom. She had plenty of money saved up, so finances would never be a problem. She smiled to herself. Life without Fred was going to be absolutely wonderful.

***

Eve Yardley-Henderson was furious. Her plans were now shot to pieces. No House of Commons soirees, no Mayfair or Downing Street address, no shopping trips to Paris and New York, no holidays in the Caribbean. And all because Doug couldn't keep it in his trousers. Well, if he expected her to play the supportive wife, he was in for a shock. He could rot in gaol for all she cared. Still, she had plenty of her own money. There was always that.

May, 2021

Carol Sharpe was sitting at her desk in the Serious Fraud Office. There was a knock at her door. Looking up, she saw Greg. She waved him in.

"Good morning," he greeted her. "I have some news for you. The trials of Douglas Yardley-Henderson, Christiana Morleigh aka Christine Muriel Mullan, Fred Denton and Jeremy Fisher are going to be held at the Old Bailey. As you know, no bail was applied for with the exception of Fisher but his application was denied."

"Excellent news, Greg. Do we have a date yet?"

"No, not yet but I suppose it'll be towards the end of the year. Will you attend?"

"Depends on the workload. I'd like to, though."

"There's just one other thing. One of the forensic accountants was going through Yardley-Henderson's finances. She discovered that his wife had accompanied him on his trips to Moscow and Tirana." Carol looked at him.

"Are you thinking what I'm thinking, Greg?" He grinned back at her nodded.

"I think we need to pay Eve Yardley-Henderson a visit. I'll ring DCS Grey and, perhaps, you could get one of the boys to start going through all her finances. With a fine tooth comb."

"Will do."

***

"Mrs Yardley-Henderson, good afternoon. I'm Detective Chief Superintendent Grey, Norssex County Police, and this is Detective Chief Inspector Gordon from the Stonechester force. May we come in?"

"I remember you all from when you raided my home. You made an awful mess." Eve said. "What do you want?"

"We have a couple of questions, that's all. May we come in?" Eve looked at them with contempt.

"Is she joining us?"

"I'm from the Serious Fraud Office," explained Carol Sharpe. "And my colleague here is from the National Crime Agency. We have a search warrant."

"What! Again!" Eve was furious. "Come in then." They trooped through into the drawing room. Eve sat down but she didn't invite them to join her.

"Mrs Yardley-Henderson," DCS Grey began. "Going through your husband's business records, we picked up that you went with him to Moscow and Tirana in 2017 and 2018, respectively. Why?" She regarded him, scornfully.

"Why not?"

"I can understand you accompanying him to Moscow, but Tirana is hardly a mecca for tourism." Eve shrugged but said nothing. Carol regarded her, those black eyes unblinking.

"Mrs Yardley-Henderson, we have reason to believe that, like your husband, you have been assisting in international money laundering, in your case, for an Albanian OCG, albeit in quite a small way. That's why we didn't pick it up, initially. We have now gone through all your own bank accounts and have found various transactions that can only be termed dubious."

"How dare you, you bitch!" Eve's face was red with anger – and fear. There was a ring at the front door. DCI Gordon got up to answer it. He returned with another man.

"Mrs Yardley-Henderson, this gentleman is from MI6. He wishes to ask you some questions." Eve's face blanched. The man sat in the armchair opposite her, uninvited. He regarded her impassively a few moments before asking, "How long have you been working for the Russian Foreign Intelligence Service?"

***

The *Stonechester Gazette* and *Norbrough Chronicle* had been carrying full details of the arrests made following the murder of Sonia Bailey. Terry Bailey, despite his editor's offer of compassionate leave, was determined to continue reporting on her murder and the arrests. He found it cathartic and helped him in his grief. He and Sonia had never really been close, but she was still his sister and he wanted to see justice done.

The citizens of the Pyddelhams and Stonechester were shocked by the murder and the arrests, especially that of Eve Yardley-Henderson for spying. As Mike

Culverhouse pointed out to Mandy, that's why she was pushing for her husband to become MP and networking and chatting up the great and good in government, both locally and nationally. It was to get information to pass on to the Russians.

These affairs formed the main subject of conversation at the Cat and Cradle, and Len Sharman was delighted to see his establishment become the main venue for all the talk and gossip and, consequently, rumours. Financial loss, due to the lockdowns, was forgotten; he was, as somebody cynically observed, bloody coining it.

Rita was more compassionate. As she remarked to Mandy Culverhouse, money was certainly the root of all evil if it drove one woman to kill another and dump her body in a reed bed. Mandy agreed and they both attended a special Sunday remembrance service at St Agatha's that Reverend Fuller had arranged to celebrate Sonia's life. Once the Coroner had released her body, her funeral had taken place in one of the chapels at Norbrough Crematorium. However, Reverend Fuller had contacted Terry and asked his permission to hold this special service at St Agatha's. Terry, overwhelmed by such kindness and thoughtfulness, had agreed. He had also been overcome by the number of people who attended; he had cried on Sara Rollins's shoulder throughout the service.

A couple of people in the congregation noticed the empty Fryers-Faversham pew and wondered where Sir Henry and Lady Caroline were.

June, 2021

"Mandy, it's me!" Rita was excited about her news and shouted into her mobile.

"Hiya! What's wrong?"

"Nothing. Oh, Mandy, guess what? The planning respecter is going to hold a pubic enquiry. About all that warehousing and supermarket and stuff."

"Er, Rita, I think you mean inspector and public enquiry. There's quite a difference, love."

Rita ignored the correction and flowed on, "Mandy, this is where we get to say no. Properly. Officially and that. I'm ever so pleased."

"When and where, Rita?"

"Later this month in the Stonechester council offices. You know, at the back of Church Lane. In Stonechester."

"I know, Rita. I'll *WhatsApp* everyone and let them know. Calm down, love."

"I can't, Mandy. I'm so pleased that the PVP get to tell them to duck off. I want to stop them building on the wold. It's where me and Len did it for the first time, and it was the first time I had an organism."

"Rita!"

Rita had the grace to blush.

"Sorry, Mandy, but we finally get to tell them people to leave the land alone."

***

Rita Sharman was correct. The planning inspector began the public enquiry at the end of June, 2021. He heard all the arguments and protests and saw various deputations and the on-line petition, the latter attracting thousands of signatories. The recent discoveries of the Great Crested Newts and the ruins, together with the recent arrests, were also taken into consideration.

September, 2021

"We've won! We've actually won!" Mandy was ecstatic.

"Tell me, tell me!" Rita begged, nearly dropping her mobile into a sink full of soapy water in her excitement.

"The planning inspector said that the warehouses were too big and would not provide sufficient high-quality jobs. However, he did agree to four acres of the Tilley land being used for solar panels which would benefit the Pyddelhams. He said his decision has been driven by the beauty and history of the land, as well as by the diversity of the wildlife. He has specifically mentioned that the mere and surrounding land must be maintained as a wildlife sanctuary and that the Saxon church and burial grounds, and some Roman finds that Historical England have revealed during excavations, must be kept sacrosanct for future generations."

"Oh, thank God!" Rita exclaimed.

"He ruled that there is, therefore, no need for a supermarket and that the Pyddel Valley must be kept exactly as it is since it is an area of outstanding natural beauty and wildlife and offers the opportunity for the people of Stonechester to enjoy it."

"There is justice, then. At last!"

"He also added that Ted Drage's buildings could become a wildlife study centre and also a museum for the finds Historical England has discovered during their excavations."

***

The ruins turned out not to be Saxon but were the remains of a small twelfth century Norman motte and bailey castle. However, following the geo-phys exercise, a large area of post holes in the ground nearby had been revealed by some exploratory trenches. These were most likely the remains of a wooden Saxon church. Burials had also been found nearby whose skeletal remains were carbon dated and found to be from the early tenth century. Members of the Stonechester Historical Society spent most of their time helping Historical England with the dig, either on their knees, trowels in hand or washing and logging the discoveries. As Susan Sudborough joyfully remarked, it was just like being on *Time Team.*

***

The Sunday after the ruling by the planning inspector, people flocked to St Agatha's. The PVP website and *Facebook* page had announced a thanksgiving service to be presided over by the Reverend Michael Fuller. He and Barbera were thrilled to see so many people attend. Once again, it was noticed that the Fryers-Favershams were missing but nobody cared, and people sat in their pew.

After the service, Reverend Michael asked Mandy and Rita to say a few words to the congregation. After their initial surprise at being asked to do so, Mandy spoke first, "I just want to thank everyone for their support in our campaign. We couldn't have done it without you all. However, there are a couple of people who, I believe, deserve special thanks and attention. First of all, Kevin Miller. Kevin did all the IT stuff for us, and it helped our campaign go nationwide. Take a bow, Kevin."

Kevin stood up to a round of applause. He smiled briefly and then sat down beside his mum.

"Secondly, I wish to thank Brian Ramsbottom and his twitchers and birders. Whatever the weather, ladies and gentlemen, they were up on the wold and down along the Pyddel Valley, keeping an eye on things each and every day, letting us all know what was happening. They also discovered the Great Crested Newts. Thanks, Brian."

Brian stood up, as did about ten others, including Fred Smith and Geoff Tunstall. They received a big round of applause and sat down full of smiles. Lorraine gave Brian a hug when he sat down.

"Thirdly, the Stonechester Historical Society. Without the discovery of our Norman ruin, the remains of a Saxon Church and burial ground, I believe we may have struggled to obtain the decision we did from the planning inspector."

All the members rose in their pew as one, grinning from ear to ear, as everyone else applauded them.

"Last, but certainly not least, I'd like to thank the Stonechester and District Wellbeing Walkers Club for all their support. In fact, really, I should thank everyone because, well, we all came together to fight for what we believe in and that's our beautiful countryside." With that, everybody in the church applauded again. Mandy said quietly to Rita, "Do you want to add anything, Rita?"

"No, Mandy. You said it all. There's nothing else to say." Mandy smiled fondly at her.

"Yes, there is, Rita. You've been a terrific support and friend. Thank you."

December, 2021

Reverend Michael Fuller was preparing his Christmas services. He thought back to this time last year. How different it had been then. He felt optimistic about the future. St Agatha's had been full every Sunday since the thanksgiving service in September. As a chirpy Winnie Jenkinson remarked to Barbera, "Lordy, me duck, I ent never seen it so full 'cept when the war was over and the Queen got crowned."

***

The members of the Stonechester and District Wellbeing Walkers Club were up on the wold. It was one of those crisp winter days, bitterly cold but with a sun shining down from a cerulean blue sky. They had all met, as per usual, in Lower Pyddelham, parking their cars along the road outside the Lodge which now sported a 'For Sale' sign. Mandy and Rita led them beside the river, still flowing gracefully through the valley, and then up onto the wold. They all wandered over to the Historical England excavations and had a chat with Susan Sudborough and Clare Capps who showed them around the site and some of the finds. June Packwood couldn't be there today, Clare explained, as she had a touch of lumbago, probably from all that digging.

Susan and Clare took great delight in showing them the post holes which, it transpired, June had discovered whilst excavating one of the trenches with her trusty trowel.

"They are pretty certain these might be for a wooden Saxon church, but the archaeologists still want to dig some more," Susan explained. Both she and Clare stood in the trench and stared in awe at the muddy ground. The Wellbeing Walkers stood along the side of the trench looking down at the holes in silence. As nothing seemed to be happening, after a time, the Wellbeing Walkers moved off, calling their goodbyes, leaving Susan and Clare still in raptures in their trench.

"I can't get excited over a pile of rubble, some bits of metal and holes in the ground, can you?" Rita murmured to Mandy.

"No, I can't either but, obviously, they can. Don't let's knock it, though. All that helped saving all of this."

They made their way around the mere before turning back towards the path to the valley. Rita stopped and regarded the scene below them. It was really quite beautiful.

"Look at the view," she called to the others. "Look at the view." Mandy thought she sounded like one of the pigeons coo-ing in her garden but she did look, as did the rest of the Walkers.

"This is what we fought for," said Rita. "To walk here and see this." Mandy nodded and said, "It's beautiful whatever the season. We are so fortunate to have all this on our doorstep." They stood looking a little longer and then descended the path back down into the Pyddel Valley. It was going to be a wonderful Christmas and New Year.